# Wager

*By the Same Author*

Hunter's Stand

# Wager

Steven Linder

**Walker and Company**
**New York**

Copyright © 1986 Steven Linder

All the characters and events portrayed in this story are fictitious.

First published in the United States of America in 1986 by the Walker Publishing Company, Inc.

Published simultaneously in Canada by John Wiley & Sons Canada, Limited, Rexdale, Ontario.

**Library of Congress Cataloging-in-Publication Data**

Linder, Steven.
   Wager.

   I. Title.
PS3562.I51118W3    1986   '   813'.54      85–29528
ISBN 0–8027–4061–8

Printed in the United States of America

10 9 8 7 6 5 4 3 2 1

*For Gene and Virginia,*
*whom I love and admire.*

# CHAPTER 1

"YOU Wager?"

"That's right."

"We got something to talk about."

Sam Wager looked up at the two men standing over him. Big men with hard-edged faces, squinty eyes that had seen hours of sun and wind. They both wore black long-tailed coats, clean white shirts, and boots shined to the gleam of dark silver. Starched and proper, the sort of clothes only bankers in that part of Montana wore. But bankers didn't wear Colt revolvers beneath their long coats, at least not the ones Wager had met.

"How 'bout it, you willing to listen?"

Wager motioned to the chairs across the table. They both sat down. "Let me figure how to start," the first one said.

"You got names? That's a good place."

"Sure. My name's Ben Lawson." The man stroked his beard as he spoke, a dark bush that masked any expression that might sneak across his face. "And this here is my partner, Tom Price." His partner blinked when his name was spoken; that was as much life as he'd shown so far. He was even bigger than Lawson, with a square jaw flat on shoulders large enough to look natural on a steer. The stubble on that block chin made Wager guess they'd been riding three or four days.

They stared at one another awkwardly. No one offered to shake hands.

Lawson broke off, glancing around the saloon. "Nice place you hang around in, Wager," he said, in the same tone he might use to say looks like it's gonna rain real soon. He sneered at the Oriental silk panels along the walls, the crimson brocades

1

and paper dragons hanging from the ceiling. "Looks like some kinda Chinese whorehouse."

"I wouldn't know," Wager said. "Never been in one myself."

"What's the matter? Don't you like whores?"

Wager frowned. "Got nothing against them. I'm sure, for instance, that your mother was a nice enough lady."

Lawson snapped his eyes back to Wager's face. He considered what he saw there for a long moment. At last he sighed and said: "Any chance we can get a drink?"

"All it takes is money."

Lon Do was in his usual position behind the bar, doing the morning's inventory. Wager raised his hand and signaled. The small dapper man put down his ledger and came straight over.

"Good morning, Sam." After ten years in America, Lon Do had shortened his bow to a brief nod of the chin. "Can I get something for you?"

"Some coffee for me, Do."

"Very good." Do nodded in turn at Lawson and Price. "And for you gentlemen?"

The two men exchanged confused looks. They stared at Do as if they didn't believe their eyes. The Chinaman smiled back evenly, a slight glow of mischief in his definitely non-Oriental blue eyes. His five feet of New-York-tailored splendor made their banker suits look like rags. As if to make sure they noticed, Do stuck his thumbs into the pockets of his waistcoat, chiming a rattle from three shiny gold watch chains.

Lawson's lip curled up as if he had something stuck in his teeth. "Forget it. I don't want nothing from no Chinaman."

Do's smile faded. Wager broke in quickly. "Never mind, Do. They're leaving anyway."

Price spoke up for the first time then. He looked at Wager and said, "Huh?"

Lawson sighed, "All right, all right. Bring us two beers."

Do waited for Wager's nod of agreement, then moved off behind the bar. Wager watched the little man until he was out of earshot; then he turned back to the two strangers. "Just so we understand each other—that Chinaman can buy and sell you ten times over. But more important, he's my friend."

"Hey, we bought drinks, didn't we?"

"Yeah, and there's a nice table over there in the corner where you can enjoy them."

A fire flickered in Lawson's eyes. He started to say something, but Do returned with the drinks then, and the big man clamped his mouth shut with a small audible click.

Do put down two beers and Price's face lit up. He grabbed a foaming mug and emptied it in one long swallow. He was wiping his lips with a sleeve while Lawson was still digging money from his pocket. He stared longingly at his partner's beer. Lawson moved a protective hand around his mug without seeming to think about it. He didn't bother to pick it up.

"You ready to talk business now?"

"I doubt you two are in any business that would interest me." Wager sipped at his coffee.

"You got something against money?"

"Actually, it's one of my favorite things," Wager said. "But this is the first time you've mentioned it."

"You are interested, then?"

"Say what you've got to say."

Lawson took a swig of beer, wiped the foam from his beard. "All right, it's nice and simple, really. We got this job we want you to do for us."

"Doing what?"

Price leaned over and jabbed a finger at Wager's face, as if to announce it was his turn to speak. "You know a man named Johnson? Wolfer Johnson, they call him; he lives about four miles from here."

"Up on White Man Mountain—sure, I know who he is. But I don't see him around much. He keeps to himself."

"Yeah, that's the man. Well, we got a box we want you to deliver to him."

"What's in it?" Wager asked.

"That's not your concern."

"So take it yourselves, then."

Price said hesitantly, "No, we'd rather not see him. He don't like us much."

Wager barely knew Wolfer Johnson, but his opinion of the man just went up a notch.

"So, are you interested?"

Wager pushed his chair back from the table, both to get comfortable and to make sure Price didn't stick a finger in his face again. "Let me try to get this straight," he said. "You want me to deliver a box to someone who doesn't like you. Who maybe *hates* you, seeing as the trouble you're going to to avoid him. Now, I'm not the smartest man in the world, but even I can figure whatever's in this box, Johnson won't be too happy to see it. No matter who brings it."

The two men looked at each other for a moment; then Lawson nodded. "All right, Wager. It's true. He's liable to get sorta upset when he sees this."

"Surprise, surprise."

"That's why we want someone he knows—at least somebody he's seen around—to take it on out there. You don't have to worry; he'll know you got nothing to do with it."

Wager lit a cigar. "What's in the box?"

"His son."

Wager studied the two of them closely, but their stone faces weren't giving away a thing. "Yeah, I can see how that might disturb him."

"How about it?"

"Why come to me about this? We got an undertaker here in Sheridan. Get him to deliver the body; this is more in his line."

"We asked him already," Price said. "He was too busy. Workin' over a couple of kids . . . makin' them pretty for looking at, you know."

"The Shannon twins," Wager said, remembering then. "Small-pox. A real shame, they were only ten or twelve years old, I think."

"Yeah, that's real sad, Wager. But all we care about is getting that box out to Johnson."

"Why'd you pick me to ask?"

Price shrugged those massive shoulders. "We asked around town for someone who wasn't doing anything. Every person we asked gave us your name."

"Oh."

Lawson laughed. "Nice reputation you have, Wager. Nobody seems to know just what it is you do. They all said that you don't do nothing."

"Not as easy as it sounds, you know."

"A person who don't do nothing could probably use some easy money."

"True. What are you paying?"

Price glanced once around the saloon. "One hundred dollars," he said.

Wager's eyes widened despite himself. "That's a lot of money."

"You want the job or not?" Lawson asked impatiently.

"No."

"No?"

"No," Wager said. "What I want is the hundred dollars."

# CHAPTER 2

THE weekly stage was in, dropping off parcels of mail and one or two weary-looking passengers who looked in a hurry to be somewhere other than Sheridan. None of the people milling about on the street paid Wager or the two strangers any mind. Their buckboard was in front of the harness shop, right across from Do's Little Shanghai. The team looked combed and fresh, and Wager recognized one of the horses as belonging to Lew Dawson, the smithy who ran the local livery.

Wager peered in the back. The box was in the bed, hidden beneath a pile of old blankets. He frowned when he saw the size of the covered crate. Before Lawson and Price realized what he was about, he put one boot on a wagon spoke, climbed up, and pulled the blankets away for a better look.

"Hey, what do you think you're doing?"

"What's this mean?" Wager said, glaring down at the two men.

"You got a problem?"

"This box—is just a box."

"That's what we told you it was."

Wager stepped down, shaking his head. "You told me Johnson's son was in it. I expected a coffin. At least something more coffinlike."

"Well, this is what you get," Lawson said, while Price stepped up and hurriedly pulled the blankets back over the small wooden crate.

"You couldn't squeeze a five-year-old in that thing."

"Not so loud, all right?" Lawson glanced furtively up and down the street. "There's no cause to get folks riled up over this."

6

"How old was he, for chrissake?"

Lawson fidgeted a bit, glanced over at his partner. Price just shrugged. "Okay," Lawson said softly. "You were pretty near right—he was about five, near enough."

"How'd he die?"

Price motioned for them to step away from the wagon. The stage was taking off again, and people were starting to wander past, returning to their normal business. Lawson and Price were acting nervous about keeping their particular business secret. Wager let them steer him a few buildings down, to the chairs set out on the boardwalk in front of the Drydall Hotel. It was a place where men commonly gathered to sit and smoke and shoot the breeze. None of them felt like sitting.

"How did the boy die?" Wager demanded again.

"He stepped in front of a train."

"Whereabouts?"

"On the tracks, of course."

"No, what town?"

"Oh." It took Lawson a second or two to reply. "Miles City, it was."

"How come you're doing this?"

"We've already been through all that."

"No, I mean why you? How did you get involved in bringing the boy home to Johnson?"

"It's just a job to us, too," Price said. "The company sent us. We're with the railroad."

Wager's eyebrows arched, a hard smile forming. "Yeah? You'd know Old Nig then. He's been with railroad out that way for a long time. How's he doing these days?"

The two men exchanged a quick look. "Well, I never knowed him that well," Price said. "But I hear he's still around, and doing all right, I s'pose."

Wager nodded, apparently satisfied. In truth, he was—for now he knew beyond any doubt that they were liars. Anyone who'd been even near the railroad crews would have known Old Nig was the horse that pulled the wagonload of ties and rails they used to lay tracks. The horse had gained local fame for pulling its load all the way from Bismarck to the junction of the railroad's western division at Gold Creek in Montana.

These men weren't railroaders any more than Wager's Aunt Martha was. And even she was a better liar.

"The company's just trying to do the decent thing," Lawson said. "It don't look good when folks hear about little boys being run over and all, so we just want to keep it all quiet. The Northern Pacific wants to see things put to rest."

"So to speak," Wager offered.

"Right. All done in a right proper way."

"I see. You and the company are doing Johnson a favor."

"Sure." The men nodded in unison.

Wager smiled thinly. "Now let's hear about *why* Johnson doesn't like you."

Price snarled and curled his hand into a fist. "Look, you want to make a hundred dollars or you want to make trouble?" he hissed. He looked fully ready to take Wager apart, piece by piece.

"Well?" Lawson asked, his voice soft and low.

"I don't know. I'm still deciding."

"You decided already, you bastard. We made a deal, and you're not backing out now."

The threat in his voice was clear enough. The threat in his hand even more so. Real nice and casually, Lawson had slipped his hand inside his coattail and rested it on the butt of his gun. Wager noted this and scowled. He knew there was nothing casual about the pose. He had more than a good suspicion now about how these two really earned their living.

Lawson saw the realization in Wager's eyes, and he smiled. "You can leave any time now," he said gently.

"Not until I see my fifty dollars."

Lawson blinked. "Your what?"

"The first half of the money now. I'll collect the rest when the job's done."

"We didn't agree on that sorta deal."

"Okay, I'll take it all now, if you'd rather pay just once."

"Hold on," Lawson growled. "You didn't say anything about money up front."

"Didn't I?"

"You know damned well you didn't."

"Funny," Wager said. "There's a lot we didn't bother to tell each other. Isn't there?"

Price grunted like a maddened bear and came at Wager. Lawson got a hand up and shoved the big man back. "Remember yourself, simmer down." He spoke softly to Price, and the big man sulkily retreated.

Wager smiled at Lawson. "Does he do any other tricks?"

The gunman scowled. "That's enough, Wager. All right, we'll do it your way. Give us a few minutes and you can have the fifty."

"That's fine. I want a little time to tell some people I'll be gone, anyway," Wager said.

"Don't tell anyone what you're doing."

"No, I won't. I just want to explain why I won't be around."

Lawson smiled. "Yeah, it must be nice to know you'll be missed."

Wager nodded, but the gunman's smile put a chill down his back. He didn't like the way that sounded, not at all.

After being outside awhile, the inside of the Little Shanghai seemed as dark and dismal as a prison cell. But a very elegant prison cell, Wager thought. He wondered if he should tell Do about Lawson's calling the place a whorehouse. The little man might enjoy the remark, seeing as how he'd bought the saloon with his inheritance, money that Mamma Do had earned operating Kat Sing, one of the most elegant and successful whorehouses in San Francisco's Chinatown.

But then, he never knew for sure how Do would take anything. For years Do had told everyone that his mother had been a Chinese acrobat whose act had so enthralled a California gold miner that he had married her and made her instantly wealthy.

A wealthy *widow*, as it turned out, for the miner's heart had not been up to Mamma Do's devotions. Wager had often suspected that part of Do's story could be true—for considering the list of services on Kat Sing's menu, acrobatics was a skill that might have come in very handy.

Still, Wager decided on caution and kept Lawson's remark to himself. He walked up and rested his elbows on the felt-top bar counter. "Pull out a bottle of that French brandy, will you?"

Do frowned. "What is it, Sam? You do not usually drink in the morning." He brought up a bottle and tumbler, set them on the counter. "Is this perhaps something to do with your new friends?"

Wager poured himself half a glass of the smoky amber liquid. "I don't know what to call them, but it's certainly not 'friends.' They've got me involved in something, and it smells like trouble."

The Chinaman nodded sagely. "I could tell they were not men to be trusted."

"How do you see that?"

"The one with the beard has crooked teeth. In China, we know that a man with crooked teeth cannot tell the truth. You must be careful of him, Sam."

Wager smiled. "You've been an American a long time now, Do. You're not supposed to believe things like that anymore."

"I know you laugh," Do sighed. "But the ways of my people are old and very wise."

Wager knocked back his brandy, shuddering a little as the warmth shot down his throat. "Speaking of old," he said, "you know Wolfer Johnson, don't you, Do? He comes in here from time to time."

"We have spoken."

"How old would you say he is?"

"This is an odd question, Sam."

"C'mon, how old you say?"

Do wiped a bar rag across a tiny spot on the counter as he thought it over. "He is eighty, eighty-five years, I believe."

Wager put his boot up on the brass rail and leaned farther across the bar. "Do you think it's possible for an old guy like that to have a five-year-old son?"

A light sparkled in Do's blue eyes. "An old man with young wife dies very stubbornly."

"Yeah, right," Wager said, unsatisfied.

"But Wolfer Johnson, he has no young wife."

Wager looked up. "You're sure?"

Do nodded. "This I know. He has lived alone many years. We have spoken of this, he and I. The woman he loved died a long time ago, and he has sought no other. There is in him, I think, a great sadness." Do shook his head. "I do not understand this—it is not wise for a man to love but one woman."

Wager stared down at his empty glass for a moment as if contemplating this. Then he looked up and met the little man's eyes. "I need a favor, Do. I want the night off."

Do frowned. "The stage has been through with the payroll boxes. Tonight we will have men from the mining and logging camps, eager to spend their wages. It will be very busy, and the men will become very drunk. The sharpers will be tempted."

"I know," Wager said. "I wouldn't ask if it wasn't important."

Do pulled out the largest of his three gold watches and studied its face, a habit whenever he was weighing a difficult question. After a minute he sighed and snapped the watch closed. "Very well. This is the first time you have asked such a thing in all the time we have worked together. I cannot refuse you this small favor."

"I appreciate it, Do." Wager put his hand around the bottle, then stopped himself and reluctantly pushed it away. "I'd better not, I guess."

"I am worried for you, my friend. This trouble you smell, it is bad?"

"I really don't know," Wager said. "I don't know much of anything, and that's what bothers me."

Do plucked an orange from the basket of fruit he kept for mixing the fancy cocktails some of the cattlemen favored. "I will eat this today, Sam, and I will scatter the peels outside your door. In the Canton province it is known that the color orange brings good fortune. Luck will be with you on this thing you must do. If you are careful, the trouble you fear will pass."

Wager smiled. "You know I don't believe in luck." He turned to leave, then hesitated and looked back over his shoulder. "But what the hell. If you're hungry enough, Do . . . eat two, will you?"

Wager kept feeling the money in his pocket, as if to convince himself he had a reason for doing what he was doing. It didn't help all that much.

The buckboard was fairly new, the wheels well greased, so it didn't creak and groan as much as most wagons do. It rode smooth and quiet—just as, Wager thought, a funeral wagon ought to. Isolated patches of snow glittered in the sun, but mostly the going was mud, black quicksand that sucked at the wheels and clung in sloggy cakes to the horses' limbs. The horses were fresh and pulled well, seeming to enjoy the exercise; once they were clear of town and onto the dryer slopes of the foothills their heads came up and they pushed themselves on at a good clip without any coaxing.

Wager could understand the horses' good spirits, for it was a clear April day, as near perfect as a body could hope for. A faint bite to the air was a reminder of winter's grim stubbornness, but the wind had eased back, gently whistling in the draws, and overhead the sun burned warm in a cloudless sky the color of storybook seas. Wildflowers were appearing, dotting the dark spaces between the holdover snows, yellow daisies, purple hyacinths, and the white brilliance of mariposa lilies, all intermingled, clusters of color loosely woven in a pattern that ran from one edge of the sky to the next. Wager kept swiveling his head, looking one way, then another, hungry to soak it all in. The real beauty of those fragile colors was something a man could appreciate after the long gray purgatory of a Montana winter.

The horses paced themselves well without any urging from him, so Wager leaned back, tilting his face to the sun. He felt like a snake that had just shed an old skin, all loose and alive, itching to move.

But he could lose himself in the beauty of the day for only so long. It seemed an inappropriate time to be feeling so alive, considering the cargo he was hauling. He mulled that thought over for a mile or two, toyed with it, tried to push it aside, but never quite succeeded. After he'd thought about it long enough, he reined in the horses and went about learning just what kind of cargo it truly was.

He found an iron crowbar in the toolbox and climbed up in the wagon bed. Pulling back the blankets, he stared down at the simple wooden crate. His mind groped for a reason not to do what he knew he must. There was no way it would get any easier, so finally he drew in a breath and set to work. The crate was nailed shut tight as a bank safe, but a few minutes of concentrated sweating and swearing were enough to loosen the lid. He pushed off the top, and sunlight streamed inside the box.

Wager sucked in his breath. There was a boy in there, all right. He had been a handsome child once, but he wasn't easy to look at anymore. The undertaker had done what he could, but there's no way to make death look right on the face of someone that young. The boy's skin was the pallor of day-old snow, smeared with a pasty powder that here and there slopped over onto long, dark hair. The hands were folded together across his chest, the fingers looking gnarled and wrinkled, as if they belonged to someone who'd lived a lot longer than this boy had ever had the chance to.

Wager didn't spend much time looking at the hands, though. It was hard for him to look away from the neat little hole in the center of the boy's forehead. A hole only a bullet could have made.

Other things were curious, too. For one, the body didn't smell much. Puzzlement got the better of him, and Wager gulped down the lump in his throat, leaned in for a closer look.

The boy didn't look filled-in quite right. Gently, Wager poked at the chest with the end of the crowbar. It sank in.

The lump in Wager's throat tasted nastier the second time it rose. He backed away, closing his eyes as if trying to shut out the entire world. Numbed, he sat on the edge of the wagon frame, paying no attention to where he was, and nearly tipped himself over onto the ground. The narrow board cut into his thighs, but he didn't notice the discomfort. When, finally, he opened his eyes again, he stared at the sides of the wooden crate, not daring to raise them to the thing inside.

Somebody had *stuffed* him. Hollowed the boy out and refilled him with cotton waste, or rags or old clothes or something. Wager didn't want to know exactly what.

It took him even longer to replace the lid than it had to open it. His hands shook so much he could barely hit the nails. Once the task was finally finished, he scrambled up on the wagon seat to get that box behind him and out of sight.

He lit a cigar to fight the sour taste in his mouth. It took three matches to get it lit. His hand still shook like a palsied old man's.

Wager had seen a few dead men before, more than one or two in the act of dying. But never had he witnessed a death so downright ugly. Maybe it was the unfairness that struck him, the plain wrongness. The sadness of a stolen life, the utter waste. Or maybe it was that he knew it had to be something called murder. Which pretty much means *all* those things.

Whatever the feeling was, he knew it would haunt him for a long time to come. The wind was still faint, but suddenly he felt cold, chilled to the marrow, as if winter had sneaked in behind him and stroked his spine with an icy finger. The chill settled deep.

But the strongest feeling was a festering rage. Men who would perform such abominations on the body of a child were inhuman, even lower than the buzzards and coyotes, cowardly creatures who slunk in the shadows, waiting to feed on the dead.

And those same men were trying to use him to carry out their low-handed scheme. God only knew what they were getting him into. The thought of being manipulated and included in such barbarousness made Wager ill, set an ulcerous fury churning in his gut.

His hand found the blood money in his pocket. The temptation was strong to ride back into Sheridan and toss it in the two men's faces. And if they tried to bring him down for crossing them, then so be it. He would welcome the fight.

*And he would end up dead.*

That was the truth of it, and there was no way around it. The sobering facts had to be faced. Lawson and Price were gunslingers, hired killers—about that, Wager had no doubts. And the odds, any way you looked at them, still came down to two to one. Against. Not good, certainly not odds to stake your life on.

Wager respected odds. He'd seen enough and done enough to learn about such things. He'd learned most from watching other men fall, men who had failed to learn the one essential truth—you can't cheat the odds. You can cheat all sorts of men; the ones who are ignorant of the odds, or disregard them, are almost begging to be cheated. They place their faith on hunches or, even worse, in something called luck. Not realizing that there are odds on luck, too, that must be respected.

The odds on luck are fifty-fifty. *Always.* Never worse, but never better. A simple flip of a coin, yes or no, heads or tails, win or lose.

Live or die.

Wager had a chance he could face Lawson and Price, and walk away. But chances were better that he wouldn't.

Simple as that.

And even if he succeeded in this act of rebellion, he still

wouldn't be much ahead. He still wouldn't know what it was all about.

If he was going to risk his life in any way, he sure as hell wanted a reason. He wanted to know why.

He sat there a long time, turning it all over and over in his head. The mystery of it was enough to give him a headache. Wager didn't like mysteries. All he knew for certain was that the men who had sent him were liars and killers who, if he turned back now, would use him for target practice without batting an eye.

That was as far as logic took him, but it was far enough. There was only one sensible course of action, and that was to move on. His only prayer for getting to the bottom of it all lay with Wolfer Johnson himself. The old man was the only one who might have some answers. There was at least a fifty-fifty chance that Johnson would feel like sharing some of those answers with Wager.

Maybe he'd get lucky.

# CHAPTER 3

WOLFER Johnson was supposedly one of the original mountain men. It was rumored that he had explored the territories alongside men like Jedediah Smith, Bridger, Colter, and Bowie. Men who had tramped into the wilderness with a compass and a lust for adventure, alone in a strange new land, armed with gun and knife and, most important, with a boundless resource of courage. Men who created history with each step they took deeper into the unknown expanse of the western continent. And Johnson, it was claimed, had been with them each step of the way.

Wager didn't buy it for a minute. He figured Johnson's claims to be nothing more than the idle boasts of a man grown old and fearful of his own insignificance. His skepticism was not without substance—if every man he'd met who claimed to have ridden with Jim Bridger had truly done so, the early West would have been too crowded to leave room for the wind to blow.

Johnson at least, he had to admit, did not make his claims loudly or even often. He lived alone, making his home far back in the hills, and did not travel into town except when he required supplies or, once or twice a year, to mail a letter. And on one day each spring he appeared to peddle his furs. Except for these few occasions, he kept very much to himself. And, though his cabin was only about four miles from Sheridan, he was bothered by few visitors, for the path to his door was barely more than a goat's trail, traced across rocky slopes and ridges where the view to one side or another was a dizzying sheer drop.

It certainly wasn't a road meant for wagon riding. By the

time he drove through Bennett Creek and entered the shadow of White Man Mountain, Wager felt as if some giant had been beating him by swinging the buckboard against his hips and buttocks. He felt conspicuously tender, and wondered if he had turned black and blue.

The air here was clean and crisp, and Wager caught the sharp scent of Johnson's chimney smoke even before he spotted the gray plumes drifting up lazily through the curtain of dark shielding pines. He was almost there, and his relief was considerable. But while he was glad the jolting ride was nearly at an end, he equally dreaded the moment that was drawing closer. He was beginning to wish he'd taken that second drink. Being drunk wouldn't help him through the awkward confrontation to come, but it sure wouldn't hurt.

He felt a tightness in his heart growing as he grew nearer. The breeze was stiffer on these high slopes, and it muttered as it sloughed through the pines, sounding like urgent whispers among distant voices. A melancholy life noise, sad in its tone, but somehow reassuring by its very presence.

The climbing was rough here as they moved up the mountain's southern face. Wager found a rutted trail and turned the team onto it, urging them into a stand of larch. He was not a tracker, or he might have noticed how crisp were the edges of those ruts, how moisture still shone along the bottoms. But he did not see these things, so he was unprepared for the surprise when they pushed through into a clearing on the other side of the trees, and there before him was the wagon responsible for the ruts. Startled, he reined in the horses and stared at the unexpected sight.

It was a simple two-wheeled cart, the sort peddlers use to carry their wares. The horses harnessed to the cart were standing idly, nosing the earth in an effort to turn up the young grass shoots. In the back of the wagon was a high pile of furs and tools and odds and ends, all lashed down tightly so no item could rub or jangle against another.

A man stood at the rear of the wagon, tugging at one of these lashings as he struggled to reach beneath the furs and retrieve something buried there. He was small, just a shade over five feet, so Wager knew it wasn't Johnson, even though the face was hidden from him. Though bowed with age, Johnson was at least a head taller than this person, whom Wager had never seen before. He sat there in the shadow of the trees, watching, wondering. He felt a certain reluctance to confront any strangers, considering the two he'd already met that morning.

The man's back was to Wager, and his hat and the collar of his Hudson coat blocked any view of his face. He seemed unaware of Wager, and as he was upwind, his horses had not caught the scent of Wager's team.

Apparently the stranger found what he was after. He took a few steps from the wagon and then went to his knees in a patch of melting snow. Wager saw now in the snow a low dark shape he had not noticed until then. He squinted but could not make out what it was. Then the stranger's hand rose, and he saw the sun flash on a long-bladed knife.

The hand arced down and blood spurted in the air, showering the snow with a crimson rain. Steam rose in a tiny cloud from the open body.

That was enough for Wager. He'd already had enough of morbid sights for one day. He grabbed up the reins and looked around for an alternate route, prepared to pass the stranger by. But a brief look around told him he was on the only trail. To the west the grove of trees continued, packed too densely for the wagon to pass. To the east was a rugged slope of scrabble and boulders the size of houses, leading to a point where the mountain fell away in a sheer cliff. Plenty of down, but nothing else.

There was nowhere to go but straight ahead. Wager snapped the reins and the team moved out into the clearing.

The man was occupied with his business, and Wager's buckboard was, after all, very quiet. Whatever the reasons, Wager found himself running right up on the stranger's cart, and still he seemed unaware he was not alone. Wager could see the thing he was laboring over now; it was a young deer. He was gutting it, splitting it open from the throat to the hindquarters. The warm blood had formed a pool in the snow, so that the deer seemed almost to be floating.

The man pulled some white powder from his pocket and sprinkled it inside the deer. Then he began intently rubbing the powder into the entrails.

Wager stopped his team behind the stranger's cart. Still the man labored on, not knowing he was being watched. Wager hoped the man wasn't the type to spook easily. He climbed down from his wagon, then stood there hesitantly, trying to come up with an innocent greeting to call out. But as he stepped near the stranger's cart, the decision was suddenly taken out of his hands. Furs in the wagon started moving, rustling frantically; then a small black head popped out. A collie dog glared at Wager, then tipped back its head and howled out a warning.

Alerted by the sound, the man spun around on his knees, knife held ready in his bloody hands. "Leave my dog alone, you son of a bitch."

Wager stood frozen, shocked by the accusation, and even more so by the realization that the man scowling at him wasn't a man at all. Very much the opposite. Beneath the wide-brimmed hat, the face that stared back at him was as beautiful as it was angry. Smooth, clear skin, a full mouth, and wide dark eyes a man could lose himself in. Even when they were flashing mad.

"What's the matter with you, mister?" she snapped. "You dumb or something?" She rose to her feet, never taking her eyes from his face. She held the knife out before her in an easy underhanded grip that spoke of her knowing how to use it. "I said get away from there."

"Sure, sure." Wager glanced at the dog, who was poised atop the pile of furs like a mountain lion preparing to strike. "Glad to. Your mutt doesn't seem to like people much."

"He likes people fine. What he doesn't like is you. He gets riled when strangers try to sneak up on me."

"I wasn't sneaking."

"Then you sure have a quiet way of saying hello."

They moved around each other like partners circling in a folk dance. As Wager moved away from the wagon, she edged closer to it. He noticed how she kept half turned so that if he lunged at her the knife would be protected until the last decisive second. Seemed like a woman who knew how to take care of herself, he thought with mixed feelings. He looked down at the deer she had been working over. "What are you doing here?" he asked, perplexed. Wager had helped his father slaughter cows and pigs back on their Fort Scott farm; this didn't look like that sort of work; if it was, it was a damned sloppy job.

While his attention was on the deer, she darted for the wagon. Hearing the quick footsteps, Wager turned back just as she pulled a rifle from under the seat of the cart. She slid the knife into a scabbard at her belt and raised the rifle in two hands, training it at his stomach.

"Now maybe we can talk better," she said.

"I thought we were doing just fine."

She gestured for Wager to lift his hands. She handled the rifle with the same ease and confidence she had shown with the knife. Wager was convinced it would not be wise to argue with her. Reluctantly, he raised his hands up around his head. "Look, we're getting off on the wrong foot here," he said. "My name's Sam Wager and I didn't mean to—"

She interrupted with a stern voice. "How nice to meet you. Open your coat, Sam Wager."

"I'm trying to be polite. You might at least return the favor and tell me your name."

She cocked the rifle. "I might. After you open your damned coat."

Wager shrugged and unbuttoned his coat. "Okay?"

"Turn around. Keep those hands up where I can see them."

Wager spun around slowly. The rifle muzzle jabbed his back. "You have a nice gentle touch."

"Shut up," she ordered. The rifle dug into his spine while she patted him down.

"I've always liked shy girls."

"I said shut up." Her hand stopped over his right-hand pocket.

"That's right; it's a gun," he said.

"How nice of you to tell me." She slipped the Colt from his pocket, and the pressure at his back was gone.

"Okay, you can come around." When Wager turned, he saw his revolver stuck in her belt, the rifle still aimed at him. A smile played at her lips, as if she was pleased with herself. She patted the grip of his Colt. "You won't mind if I hold on to this awhile," she said. "At least until I find out what you're up to."

He shrugged. "Doesn't matter. It's not loaded."

She smiled disdainfully. "Of course not. What are you grinning at?"

"I'm just a happy person. You've got to admit—this is a pretty ridiculous situation."

"I don't know what kind of situation this is," she said. "But I aim to find out. You're going to explain it to me. Starting right now."

"Sure, be glad to."

"Well? Get on with it; what are you doing here?"

Wager said, "I came to see Wolfer Johnson. That is his cabin up there on the ridge, isn't it?"

"It is," she said curtly. "What do you want with him?"

Wager hesitated. He looked at her and mugged a reluctant expression. "Don't get mad now."

"Mad about what?"

"My answer."

"Which is?"

He said, "It's none of your business."

A hard scowl settled on her face, and she raised the rifle to her shoulder.

"I'm glad you didn't get mad. What I'm saying is that my business is personal, between Johnson and me."

She studied him over the rifle sight, which was straight in line with the center of his forehead. "If it has to do with Ethan Johnson, then it's my business, too."

Wager was taken aback. "Yeah? Why is that?"

She shook her head angrily. "I'm the one asking the questions here. And you're doing a lousy job with the answers." She smiled and patted the trigger ever so gently. "Maybe a bullet would convince you to try harder."

Wager looked at her, a hard frown on his face. Then he sighed and dropped his hands. "You're right. This is getting us nowhere."

"You better raise those hands again. Fast."

"I've had enough," he said wearily. "Go ahead and shoot me."

In a snap move she lowered the rifle and jerked the trigger. The gun barked, and a small cloud of dust rose at a point between Wager's legs. He flinched and looked up, chagrined. "That was just an expression."

"You got a clearer mind on things now?" she asked.

Wager compromised and raised his hands a little way, about chest high. He gestured with one hand toward the wagon. "Look, I've got a box in that buckboard. Two men paid me to deliver it to Johnson. That's all I'm here to do, it's all I care about. You can come along and keep that gun on me the whole time if you like. But either way, I'm going up to the cabin now. If you think you have any reason to stop me, then just shoot me now and get it done with."

She wavered, doubt darkening her eyes. "What's in the box?"

"I don't know," Wager lied.

"You sure that's all you're about? You're not going to hurt him?"

Wager shook his head. "I don't want to hurt anybody."

She studied his eyes so intently he felt as if she were looking right through him. Then slowly she lowered the rifle. "All right, Sam Wager. Let's go. I'll be with you the whole time. And if you lied to me . . ."

"I'll keep it in mind," he said.

"You do that."

He walked toward the wagon, and the girl fell in behind him. He could tell from her shadow that she had the gun aimed at him again in case he turned and tried something. Smart girl.

The horses had found a few sprigs of grass and were grazing contentedly. They glanced up at Wager as if disappointed to see him back so soon. Not my day for pleasing anyone, he thought. He went up to the wagon, then stepped back and bowed chivalrously. "After you."

She scowled and motioned impatiently with the rifle. "Don't be funny. Move it."

He shrugged and flung himself up on the seat. Then, as she grabbed the side of the wagon to climb up behind him, he turned with deceptive casualness and pulled the rifle from her grip. Before she had time to get spooked, he tossed it back in the bed. "There. Now let me give you a hand up."

She glared up at him, murder in her eyes. "You go to hell."

"You have a lovely way with words."

Quickly and easily, she pulled herself up beside him. Her small frame was quivering with rage. As she sat on the board seat, she patted Wager's revolver at her belt. "Just remember, I've still got this."

"It's not loaded. I told you that."

"Yeah, sure." Before he could protest, she whipped out the gun, pointed it aside, and yanked back on the trigger.

The hammer clicked hollowly.

She frowned in disbelief, snapped it twice more.

"I wish you'd stop that. Dry firing's not good for the mechanisms."

She threw him a dirty look and tossed the gun into the back. "What's the point of carrying an empty gun?"

"Loud noises bother me."

She flopped back in the seat and folded her arms across her chest. "Oh, let's go," she said, with an air of disgust.

"Anything you say." Wager flicked the reins. The horses arched their backs and whinnied in protest, as if they didn't want to go any farther. Wager knew just how they felt.

# CHAPTER 4

WAGER steered his team around the girl's cart, and they rode on through the clearing. The girl put two fingers in her mouth and let out a shrill whistle. The horses in her team raised their heads and dutifully started to follow.

Wager said, "Well-trained animals there."

"Ethan can perform miracles with them," she said.

"You staying with him or something?"

"That's right."

"You been with him long?"

"Awhile."

"You a friend of his, or kin, or what exactly?"

She startled him with a darting wide-eyed look, almost fearful. "Why's that matter?" she asked. "What difference does it make to you?"

"Not much, really. I'm just a snoop."

She looked at him a moment, then shook her head and relaxed a little. "Yeah, I'd believe that."

Just then Wager thought of something, and he stopped the horses.

"What are you doing?" she asked.

"Going back. We forgot that deer you were working on."

"No, it's all right. I finished with it."

"You're just going to leave it there?"

"Of course," she said, and continued to look straight ahead.

Wager rubbed a hand over his face, muffling his sigh of exasperation. "I'm confused." He was upset by her stiff pose of indifference. He wished she would look at him, at least. "I don't get it. Why do you want to leave all that venison to rot in a field? Seems to me the wolves and coyotes will tear it apart before you can come back after it.''

She finally looked his way. The look of ridicule she gave him made him wish she hadn't. "That's the whole idea," she said. "How else do you think I'm going to get any wolves?''

"I still don't get it.''

She let out a little groan, then dug into her coat pocket and held out her hand to him. In her palm was a small mound of white crystals. They could have been sand or soap powder, for all Wager could tell. "Very nice," he said.

"Don't you know what these are?''

Wager smiled uncomfortably. "No.''

"You don't know much, do you? These are strychnine crystals. Poison. You do know what poison is, don't you?''

"Poison, knives, and guns. You're a real fun-loving sort of person, aren't you?'' Then he remembered her rubbing the crystals into the deer's entrails, and it became clear what she was hinting at. "You poisoned that deer, leaving it as a trap for the wolves. So when they eat it they'll get a mean little stomachache and die.''

Her smile wasn't exactly a heart-warmer. "Congratulations," she said. "You got it. I'll bet you can't wait to get home and write this down in your diary.''

"What do you have against wolves?''

The trail led them into a thick grove of ponderosa pines, and suddenly the light grew dim. The heavy-branched trees muffled all sounds, and the air was sweet, cloying. She leaned forward and stuck out an arm. "Over that way. The cabin is just the other side of these trees.''

Wager turned as directed, then looked at her and tried his question again. "Why do you want to kill wolves?''

Her chest heaved as she let out a very long sigh. Wager thought it was amazing how much air she could expel in one try. "We kill the wolves for their pelts," she said, as if talking to a child. "The hides. And then, when we have enough, Ethan goes into town and sells them.''

"There much money in that?"

She frowned, but it was more a thoughtful look than one of disapproval. Her tone had softened. "No, not that much money," she said. "There used to be a good market for furs, but not so much anymore. We still trap them, though, because . . . well, because Ethan has done it so long, and it means so much to him. It's been his whole life." Her voice had softened even more, grown warm and affectionate as she spoke of the old man. "He's been teaching me how to do it. Passing it down, like a trade, you know. He doesn't get around as well as he used to, but it's important to him to see the job still being done. I can't trap as well as he can, but I do as much as I can. It makes him feel good to see the hides stacking up."

Wager said gently, "Hey, that was nice. You almost smiled there."

She turned to him, the icy scowl very much back in place.

Wager said quickly, "Don't worry. It was just a little one." He held up his thumb and forefinger, separated by a mere fraction of an inch. "Not much. But it was nice."

"Do you talk all the time?" she moaned.

They moved through the pines down a narrow trail, in places so tight that the coarse branches rubbed noisily against the sides of the wagon. Then a burst of sunlight struck their faces, and they were through into a clearing. The densely packed trees continued around, completely encircling the space like the stockade walls around a fort. On the north perimeter of the circle was Johnson's cabin. Wager's eyes opened in an expression of puzzlement, for it was a curious structure. To begin with, it was easily twice the size of any such cabin he'd ever seen before. As big as any of those stately homes he'd seen in St. Louis, or even back east in New York. Finding, stripping, and fitting the logs required for such a structure was no small accomplishment, he thought.

On the south side was an impressive wide porch, enclosed with a railing that was just the right height for a man to kick back his chair and rest his feet on. Surrounding the house and defining a yard was a wall like the sort they have everywhere in England, about three feet high, constructed entirely of stones fitted carefully and tightly, without mortar.

But the oddest part of the dwelling was the fact that part of it lay buried. The rear portion was sunk into the hillside so that at the very back, only the roof was above ground.

Wager became aware of the girl watching him, an amused gleam in her eyes.

"What happened, did it settle like that?" he asked.

"No, Ethan dug the space out of the hillside and built it like that."

"Why? I can see how it makes the place level, but most folks do the same thing by raising one end with foundation posts."

"This way the air can't get under the floor," she said. "Ethan says the earth banked up around the walls keeps the house warmer in the winter and cooler in the summer. You see, the ground doesn't change temperature all that much, like the air does. It's something he learned during a time when he was living in a cave."

"I'll take your word for it. I never thought much about such things."

"What do you think of it?" she asked, and the pride was evident in her voice, as if she had built it all herself. "It took him years to make it like this, doing almost all of it himself."

"It's like no place I ever saw before," Wager said.

"That's what I said the first time I came here."

They pulled up outside the gate in the stone wall. Wager set the brake against the roll of the hillside and started to get down. The girl put a hand on his arm. "Let me go ahead. He doesn't see so well anymore, and he might get spooked. He's not used to visitors."

Wager nodded, dreading the moment to come when Johnson saw the box. Any delay at all was welcome.

The girl leaped down from the wagon and ran through into the yard, calling out for the old man. "Ethan, I'm back. We got company, come on out. It's okay, don't worry. It's me, Sarah.''

Wager realized it was the first time he'd heard her name. Sarah. It had a nice sound to it. She ran up to the porch with a sort of excited abandon, looking suddenly girlish, all the competent menace of a few minutes earlier vanished. Not girlish, exactly, either. Actually, what she resembled was a very attractive woman.

It had been a long time since he'd felt stirred by the sight of a woman. All the women in the frontier towns seemed to be alike. They were all either whores, dancing girls, or other people's wives. Professionals, out to make a buck, the whores were usually friendly—if somewhat cynical. The dancing girls were just plain tired. And the wives were too busy trying to get rid of the other girls to be much fun to anybody.

Sarah's footsteps plunked on the hardwood floor of the porch just as the door swung open and Wolfer Johnson stepped out into the light. Eighty years old or not, he was still a striking figure. Six feet five, with broad shoulders and a barrel chest, with hardly an ounce of fat anywhere to be seen. His hair was totally gray, but his long, full beard was streaked with black that had never faded. The dark lines of facial hair ran like frown lines, giving him a perpetual scowl, making him appear all the more imposing.

His expression when he saw the girl, though, was so warm and affectionate as to overpower his brooding countenance. He smiled from ear to ear and opened his arms to her.

"Sarah girl," he said softly. "I was wonderin' if you'd make it back today. I heard you coming up the draw, but I thought it sounded peculiar. Wasn't sure it was you. In the old days I would have known. Then I could have told you the size of your wagon, how many horses in your team, and which leg each of them favored." As they embraced, his eyes naturally wandered over her shoulders and settled on Wager, still sitting on the buckboard. The old man flinched and pushed the girl back to arm's length. "Who's that?" he demanded.

Sarah quickly put her hands at his chest as if to hold him back. "Easy, now, it's all right. He came with me. It's a man from town. Sam Wager, he said his name is."

Johnson seemed unnaturally alarmed, and all the tenderness was gone from his voice now. "What's he want here with us?"

"I don't know, he wouldn't tell me. He said it was personal business, between him and you. There's something in the wagon he's supposed to deliver here."

The old man took a deep breath. "All right, girl. I'll see to this." Gently, he pushed her aside and stepped from the porch. Before he started across the yard, he picked up a rifle that was leaning against the porch rail. The gun was an ancient Sharps .45–90, sixteen pounds of pure firepower. He rested the big gun in the crook of his arm as if it weighed no more than a feather.

"Come down here, Sam Wager," Johnson called out. "Come closer, so I can see your face."

Wager climbed down from the wagon and slowly walked into the yard until he was about ten feet from the old man. "How are you today, Mr. Johnson?" he said, with as much cheerfulness as he could muster.

"That's close enough," Johnson said coolly.

Wager stopped. He stood stock-still while Johnson blinked and tried to make out his face. Wager had trouble keeping his eyes off the Sharps rifle, a miniature cannon, really, which could stop a buffalo dead in its tracks from four to five hundred yards.

Johnson studied him for a minute, then nodded his bearded chin. "Yeah, I've seen you in town before. Around the saloons, it seems like. Heard folks mention your name once or twice, too, as I recollect. Never heard them say anything good about you, though."

"That's me, all right."

"We've never talked any business before, have we?"

"No, sir, we haven't," Wager said.

Johnson shifted the rifle to a more businesslike grip with both hands. "So what do you want with me today, Sam Wager?"

Wager licked his lips nervously. The dreaded moment. "Well, it's kind of difficult to explain."

"All right," Johnson said gruffly. "Then work at it."

Wager sighed. "Okay. I guess there's no way around it. Two strangers paid me to bring a box out here. There's something in it you're supposed to see. But I don't think you're going to like it."

Sarah edged up beside Johnson. Her hand clutched at his arm. "What is it?" she asked breathlessly.

"Well, it's not a what, exactly. . . . It's a *who*."

"Oh, God, no!"

Sarah broke and ran for the wagon. Wager raised his hands lamely to stop her, but she tore past him and was out the gate before he had even turned around. He was strongly aware of Johnson's presence behind him and could do nothing but watch helplessly as she jumped up into the buckboard and began clawing at the lid with her bare hands.

He must have done a poor job of putting the crate back together, or maybe it was just because she was so pumped up, but whatever, Sarah had no trouble tearing into it. She had the top off in seconds. She peered down at the thing inside, and all the blood rushed from her face. A trembling seized her, and her lips moved soundlessly.

Johnson stepped up, peering about in confusion. His weak eyes were unable to follow clearly what was happening. "Sarah," he called out. "Sarah, what is it, girl? Is it . . . ?"

Head lowered, she grabbed the sides of the box as if she were dizzy and about to fall. "It's Tommy," she said. Her voice was a terrible flat sound, dulled beyond pain. "It's Tommy. The bastards found him."

At his back, Wager heard Johnson give a low, strangled moan. Still, he could not take his eyes from the girl. He felt trapped, frozen, unable to move, barely even to think.

Suddenly Sarah's head snapped up, and her eyes fell straight on Wager. There was something glittering in those eyes he recognized all too clearly. "You no-good lying bastard," she hissed. "You almost took me in. Child-killing son of a bitch!"

"I'm sorry. Truly."

"Sorry!"

"Please, if you'd give me a chance to explain."

"Like the chance you gave this little boy?" Sarah snapped. In a blur of motion she leaped from the wagon and was upon him before he could shake out of his daze. She was like a wild animal, attacking totally without reservation, throwing herself through the air like a pouncing cougar. Her fingers curled into claws and raked at his eyes.

Taken off guard, Wager got his hands up too late. Her fingernails slashed at his face, missing the eye by a mere inch. Blood spurted in a long jagged line from his temple down to the cheekbone. He jerked back in pain and surprise, half blinded by stinging blood.

"Sarah!" Johnson cried out. "Get away, girl. Leave him to me."

Wager caught a glimpse of the old man approaching, waving the Sharps. But he was too busy to worry about that threat just yet.

Spurred by the sight of blood, Sarah passionately pressed the attack. She closed with him fearlessly, stung him with blows to the face and body. She was too far gone to aim, but her wild punches still scored, for she had him cornered, and he was afraid to fight back. The blood burned in his eyes, and he could not see to protect himself, could only retreat. Until he was backed up and trapped against the stone wall.

With an animal cry, Sarah came at him again. Desperate, Wager did the only thing he could think of. As she stepped in, fists flailing, he threw his arms wide and gathered her to his chest in a tight bear hug.

Trapped and pulled off balance, she fell against him, her arms pinned helpless at her sides. Wager put his mouth against her ear. "Listen to me," he gasped. "For God's sake, will you hear me out?"

She jerked her head back violently from the intimate contact. "Let them listen to you in hell, you son of a bitch!" She reared back and tried to drive her knee up into his crotch.

Wager saw it coming and yanked her off balance. He would not release her, so they spun in an awkward, dizzy circle like drunken dancers. She pulled him this way and that, trying to break free, and he had all he could do to keep his feet and contain her.

"Let me go, you bastard. Get your filthy hands off me!"

"Not until you listen to me."

"Lies! You'll kill us all." With that, she arched her back and spit in his face.

Wager's head snapped back as the spittle glanced off his neck and jaw. He smiled grimly and tightened his hold around her until he feared breaking her back. Her struggling slowed as the air was forced from her lungs. He leaned in until his face was right up against hers. For a moment he was pleased with himself, thinking that he had at least halted her cursing. Then he realized she wasn't swearing because she was about to spit again.

"Oh, no," he said, and stopped her the only way that came to mind. Which was simply to dip his head and press his lips to hers.

The kiss certainly had value in terms of sheer surprise. For a second Sarah was stunned, unable to formulate a resistance. And for that brief moment Wager was flooded with a wash of unexpected sensations. The taste of her was overwhelming, salty and yet sweet, and he could feel the whole length of her slim body caught against him and trembling. It was actually almost pleasant, certainly would have been in different circumstances, and something inside him began to stir.

Suddenly he felt guilty. At the same moment Sarah found her wits and started to bare her teeth. As he felt her teeth start to clamp down on his lip, he quickly shoved her away, spun her around, and trapped her arms behind her back so that she was caught as if handcuffed.

"There," he said, gasping for breath. "Now you can spit or do all the nasties you like. One way or another, though, you're damned well going to hear me out."

Sarah struggled, but without much strength. She was winded, blinking back tears in her frustration.

"Stop that now," Wager said. "I don't want to hurt you."

"Let me loose!"

"Oh, no. Mrs. Wager didn't raise a foolish son."

Wager had been concentrating on gripping her slippery hands. Now he looked up. He found himself staring into the muzzle of what looked like the biggest rifle he'd ever seen. Johnson was standing behind it, about five feet away. The rifle was about five feet long.

"I don't need a youngster's eyes to hit you from here," Johnson said. "You let go of my Sarah."

Johnson's hands were shaking a little, the way some old men's hands are prone to do. They were shaking awfully near the trigger.

Wager swallowed once, loudly. "Just what I was about to do," he said.

He released her. She spun around and gave him a look that almost made him wish Johnson would pull the trigger. She was too weary to attack him again, but it was clear she wanted to.

She went over and stood beside the old man, leaning on him as she caught her breath. "What are we going to do with him, Ethan?" she asked.

"I been thinking on that," Johnson said. "I think we ought to kill him."

Wager muttered, "Nope, bad idea."

Johnson went on as if he hadn't heard. "And then we could skin him open."

"I catch cold easy." Nobody was listening.

". . . Rub some strych in his entrails and then leave him for the wolves to find."

Sarah and Johnson looked at each other for a moment. Then they both looked at him. "What do you think about that, Mr. Wager?" Johnson asked.

Wager shook his head. "It's no good, it would never work."

"Why not?"

"I was a sharper for too long. And a wolf would never eat a gambler."

"Yeah? Why's that?"

Wager said, "Professional courtesy."

The old man laughed. "Say, that's pretty good, Wager. I heard the same joke once, but the way they told it, it was wolves and lawyers." He laughed some more, showing two rows of short white teeth. "I never heard it told with sharpers."

"The only difference," Wager said, "is that a lawyer always does his gambling with *other* folks' money."

Sarah stared straight ahead, unblinking, unimpressed. But the old man threw back his head and roared. "I like that, boy," Johnson said, after he had caught his breath. "You got spunk, I'll give you that. Ain't every man could stand here and make jokes while I got a gun on him." He shook his grizzled head and then peered down the rifle. "It's gonna make me almost sorry to kill you."

"Thank you, Mr. Johnson," Wager said. "You don't know how much that means to me."

# CHAPTER 5

DARK clouds had appeared from nowhere and were moving across the face of the sun. A huge shadow slithered over the mountainside, closing out the spaces of light between the clustered pines. The pathway leading off through the trees looked dark and forbidding. Wager was glad he wasn't superstitious. It seemed about as bad an omen as one could ask for.

He took his eyes from the sky and saw Sarah studying him, a quizzical look on her face. He smiled at her.

"You don't seem very upset at the idea of dying," Sarah said.

"Actually, right now my insides feel like I swallowed a stomachful of snow."

"If you're scared, it doesn't show."

"Habit," Wager said. "Something I learned a long time ago, in a different life."

She frowned. "Are you really a professional gambler?"

"Used to be. Not anymore."

"Why did you give it up?"

A dark look flashed in Wager's eyes. "That's personal," he said.

Johnson returned then and took the Sharps from Sarah. She had been holding the gun on Wager while the old man personally inspected the crate and the body of the boy they'd called Tommy. The old man's face was stiff, the eyes red, and something glittered in his beard that looked suspiciously like tears. He poked the muzzle of the rifle against Wager's chest. "All right, Sam Wager. You've got exactly one minute."

"To do what? Say my prayers?"

"If you like," Sarah said. "But you'd better use the time by talking to us. We're waiting to hear one good reason why we shouldn't kill you here and now.''

Wager thought for a second. Then he shook his head. "No," he said. "I can't do that."

"What?" the man and girl said as one. Sarah's black collie had been napping on the porch. It raised its head, alarmed by the sharp clap of their voices.

Wager was suddenly very tired. He let his arms drop to his sides.

Johnson growled, "You better get those hands up again, fast.''

Wager let out a dry laugh. "Why? What'll you do if I don't— shoot me? You're already planning to do that."

"Your time's going fast," Sarah said. "You'd better explain yourself."

Wager nodded. "What I'm saying—trying to say—is that I can't give you a good reason not to shoot me . . . because I don't have a good reason for being here in the first place." He dug into his pocket, pulled out the fifty dollars, and held the money up. "Here, this is the only reason I came out here. I didn't know anything about the boy, or about the pain it would cause you to see him. And I still don't understand any of it. Who the boy is to you, or why somebody killed him."

"You expect us to believe that you're just an innocent bystander?"

"If I had known what this would lead to, do you think I would have come at all?" Wager said. "C'mon now, do you really think I'm that stupid?" He glanced at Sarah's glowering eyes and immediately regretted putting it that way. He sighed. "Well, maybe I am. A smart man would have known better than to do business with two low-lifes like Lawson and Price."

"Who'd you say?" Sarah burst out. He saw a shudder ripple through her. She was suddenly tensed, pitched forward on her toes. "Ben Lawson and Tom Price—big men, dark clothes?"

"The same charming couple."

A curious excitement danced in Sarah's eyes. She looked at

Johnson, and he made a little motion with his hand for her to calm herself. The old man turned back to Wager. "Where'd you meet these two men, back in town?"

Wager nodded. "They came up to me outta the blue."

"And they asked you to bring Tommy out here to us?"

"No, they *hired* me to do it."

"Why'd you agree to do it?"

"For the money, of course," Wager said.

"And you decided to take the job," Sarah muttered angrily. "Even though you knew what they were up to."

"I didn't know about the boy until I had already agreed," Wager said. "And by then it was too late. The two choirboys made it clear what they'd do to me if I tried to back out. I didn't seem to have any choice."

Johnson snorted and spat in the grass. "Why didn't you just stand up to them?"

Wager smiled dryly. "Mr. Johnson, I don't know about you . . . but when I got a choice between making a hundred dollars or making myself dead, I don't have a lot of trouble with the decision."

Sarah said scornfully, "Sure. Go for the money. That's all your sort cares about, isn't it?"

Wager stiffened. He looked at Sarah, and there was a coldness in his eyes. "Girl," he said, "you don't know me nearly well enough to say a thing like that."

His voice was soft, but there was an edge to his tone that made her draw back. For a minute they all looked at one another, and no one spoke. The sky was continuing to darken, and the breeze that blew up in their faces carried a chill.

Finally, Wager threw up his hands in a gesture of frustration. "How long are you going to keep this up? Dammit, I didn't kill that boy over there. All I did was get suckered into doing the dirty work for those two back in town. They *used* me. Don't you understand that?"

Johnson said, "Yeah. Well, all we got is your word on that."

"So why the hell didn't they just come out themselves?" Wager snapped.

"Because they knew what would happen," the old man snarled. "They knew when we saw what they done to our Tommy that all hell would break loose. They'd have a shootin' war on their hands."

"Right." Wager rubbed at his eyes as if he had grown very weary. "So what do you do if you want to start a shooting war but you don't want to be in it? You send somebody else. Some poor slob who doesn't know what's going on."

"There's some sense in what he says, Ethan," Sarah said hesitantly. She took the old man's arm, as if to steady him. "Maybe he is telling the truth. After all, he doesn't seem to have much to gain."

"I don't know," Johnson mumbled. "It's all so twisty and tricky-like. Gotta have time to think it all through."

Wager nodded understandingly and leaned back casually against the stone wall, letting out a weary sigh. "Now you're starting to see sense. Let's sit down like decent folks and talk it around."

Johnson growled and stuck the rifle back up in Wager's face. "Don't you start feelin' too easy with us. I'm not ready to trust you yet, Wager."

Wager laughed tightly. "Trust me? Nobody's asking you to trust me. I don't give a damn what you think about me or anything else. I just want out, no part in this."

Sarah scowled. "That's about what I expected from you."

"Fine. I'm glad you're pleased."

Johnson touched the rifle muzzle to Wager's cheek. As a way of getting his attention, it was pretty effective. "There's one more thing," the old man said. "Look me straight in the face, Sam Wager. I want to see your eyes when you answer this. How long have you worked for Skelly?"

Wager blinked, confused by this turn. "Who's Skelly?" he asked.

"If Lawson and Price are in Sheridan, then maybe Skelly is, too. Where's he staying?"

"If I don't know who the man is, I'd have a hard time knowing if he's in town or not," Wager said.

Slowly, Johnson pulled back the rifle. "Okay, I believe him, more or less," he said to the girl. "Though where that leaves us, I still don't know."

"It's starting all over again, isn't it, Ethan?" she said, and hugged herself as if suddenly cold. There was a long silence in which they all stared at the ground, avoiding one another's eyes. The dog on the porch whimpered, baring its teeth as it kicked about in some canine dream. Overhead, clouds had completely darkened the sky, casting an eerie premature twilight, and the air was oddly still, hushed. A faint rumble of thunder echoed from the far side of the mountain.

Finally, it was Wager who broke the silence. He spoke quietly, but there was an edge to his voice as sharp as the sudden chill in the air. "All right," he said. "So what happens next? What do you want from me?"

Sarah and the old man exchanged a brief glance. "I'm not sure yet," Johnson replied after a moment. "I guess we'll hold you for a spell until we know for sure what those bastards are up to. We can't have you going back and telling them what you know."

Wager shook his head ruefully. What he knew? Anyone who could make sense of the thoughts tumbling in his head was a better man than he.

Johnson motioned toward the house. "Come on inside where we can keep an eye on you."

Wager nodded reluctantly. He pushed past the old man and started for the porch. He glanced at Sarah as she took up step beside him. He felt he should say something to her, but was damned if he knew what. The expression on her face didn't make her appear very receptive, anyway.

He had just put one foot on the porch when he saw her expression change. Suddenly her eyes widened, her attention snapping to something behind him. "Ethan?" she said, in a startled, breathless tone.

Wager saw it in her eyes. "Oh, no," he said. And then the rifle butt hammered into his skull.

Wager stared groggily at a knothole in one of the porch floorboards. He wondered how come it was so close to his face. The old man was saying something, but his voice seemed to come from a long distance away.

"You'll be a lot easier to keep an eye on if you aren't moving," Johnson said.

Wager had a few choice words to say back, but he couldn't seem to get them out. His brain felt like a sludge pond, and picking the right words out of all that mess just didn't seem worth the effort.

With a groan, Wager rolled over onto his back. He gazed up at the sky and was amazed at how dark it looked. He wondered dimly if the storm was about to hit—the clouds seemed to be moving so fast, spinning and swirling in ever tighter circles.

Then he realized the ground was spinning, too. It was getting dark as well, just like the sky. Funny kind of storm, Wager thought. It was a toss-up as to which was darker now, the sky or the earth.

And then it didn't matter because the darkness was everywhere.

# CHAPTER 6

SARAH knelt over Wager and ran her fingers through the sandy hair on the back of his head. An ugly red lump was already forming there. "You shouldn't have hit him so hard, Ethan," she said.

Johnson prodded Wager in the ribs with a toe. "He's young and strong. He won't die easy." The old man grabbed the unconscious Wager under the arms. "Grab his legs, Sarah. We'll lock him up in the root cellar. That's a good place for him."

The two of them half carried, half dragged Wager into the house and through to the rear wall, where a small door opened into a cellar cut directly into the mountainside. There were shelves clear around the earthen walls; glass jars and tin cans glittered dimly in the light of the candle Sarah lit.

"Is he still okay?" she asked breathlessly. Wager was a good-sized man, and she was winded from the effort of hauling him.

"Close enough," Johnson said. He still breathed easily; years of tough frontier life had left his body rock-hard; carrying Wager was barely exercise to him. Now, while Sarah rested, he went to the back of the cellar and groped around on a low shelf.

"What are you looking for?" Sarah went over to help him; she knew his weak eyes were all but useless in the dim light.

"Never mind, found it," he said, holding up a rusty bucket full of sprout-covered potatoes. He dumped the vegetables onto the floor and set the bucket down near Wager's head.

"What's that for?" Sarah asked.

"He's liable to be sick when he comes to. Happens sometimes when a man takes a knock on the head. It's bad enough having to watch over him. I don't fancy cleaning up after him."

"I'll get him a blanket, too. It's chilly in here."

"Don't be fussin' over him, girl," Johnson grumbled. "He ain't no proper guest."

Sarah smiled. "Ethan, you knocked him out cold. No way he'll mistake that treatment for hospitality."

"Yep, I did." The old man grinned and swooshed his fist through the air. "It felt good, too. I still got some juice in these old bones."

Sarah turned away to hide her smile. When she stepped out of the root cellar and walked down the corridor into the main section of the house, Johnson was still peering down at Wager proudly as if he were a prize buck. She went into her little bedroom, which was off the kitchen. There were few feminine frills about the room except for the bright curtains at the windows and the brushes and combs scattered on a simple nightstand. Apart from these, there was nothing in the room but a humble brass-railed bed, a dressing table and stool, and a worn, well-traveled-looking trunk. She opened the trunk and pulled out a bright red and blue comforter. She ran her fingers lovingly over the intricate hand-stitching, then started back the way she had come. Walking through the main room in the front of the house, she paused for a second, her attention drawn to the open front door as a blast of chill air barged inside. Her eyes fell naturally on the objects outside. The buckboard and that awful wooden box.

Sarah stopped in her tracks.

"Tommy." The name broke through her lips like a moan. She stood there a moment, not moving. Her eyes brimmed with moisture, and she closed them tightly, almost fiercely, as if faced with a stinging hot wind.

For a long time she stood frozen. Then she let the blanket slip through her fingers and fall to the floor.

With careful, quiet steps, she went to a cabinet on the far wall, took down a lever-action Winchester. Pulling out a drawer, she filled her pockets with the shells she found there. Then she walked outside, gently closing the door behind her.

Johnson smoked his pipe while he watched Wager slumber. He wondered what was keeping Sarah so long. He had a dozen thoughts banging around in his brain, but one idea kept coming to the fore: he had a hole to dig. He was concerned about the girl; he had to give Tommy a proper burial, and the sooner the better. The longer the boy sat around untended to, the more upset Sarah was likely to become.

He called to her several times, and scowled in frustration when he received no answer. Probably went off somewhere to cry in private, he thought. But she shouldn't be alone now.

He prodded Wager once more with a toe and received only a gentle moan for his troubles. It seemed the townsman was ready to sleep away the whole afternoon. And all because of a gentle tap on the head.

Johnson frowned down at Wager. "This is about as much fun as watchin' paint dry," he said. "And you ain't even colorful." He stuck his pipe in his teeth and went stomping down the corridor.

No Sarah anywhere. "Now where did she get off to?" he muttered as he completed his search of the house. Had to be outside. Oh, God, he thought, I hope she ain't trying to tend to the boy herself. He strode to the front door and flung it open. Walking outside, he went a little ways across the yard until his eyes could focus on the townie's buckboard. He was relieved to see Tommy's coffin still in the back and undisturbed. Then he saw that the horses were gone, the yoke and harnesses lying on the ground.

"So that's what she's up to," Johnson said to himself in a tone of disbelief. "Tendin' to the man's horses like he was an honored guest or something. Probably even feeding them some of my oats. Lord, what does get in that girl's head."

Sighing, he turned and went back into the house. He took

only a few steps into the main room before he saw the open cabinet.

Johnson stood and stared at the gun cabinet as if waiting for it to change shape, for his feeble eyes to refocus and see it close itself up. But his eyes were seeing clearly.

"No, girl, no!" He was suddenly all aquiver, the shudders going up and down his body. She wouldn't, she couldn't have.

Yet he knew it as certainly as if he had watched her go.

"Sarah, don't do this!" he cried out. "You're all there is left, girl. All there is." In frustration, he banged his hand down on a table, not even realizing that he clutched his pipe in that hand. The wooden pipe shattered, and ash and burning tobacco went flying everywhere. The old man didn't seem to notice.

He stared outside through the open door. "Dammit, girl, turn around," he sobbed.

Then he sat down and buried his face in his hands.

# CHAPTER 7

WAGER groaned softly in his near-slumber. He came to slowly, wading up through the waves of darkness. A moment later he found himself awake, but still uncertain how he felt about the fact. The air around him seemed musty and close, and the flickering glow of the candle was like a live thing that wouldn't hold still, light fighting against shadow in a war that was too frantic for his bleary eyes to settle on. He tried sitting up. Bad idea. A bolt of pain shot down his spine, and he fell back onto his side, doubling over as dizziness sent the walls spinning around him.

His hand barked against something, which toppled over and rattled with a hollow clank. The racket buffeted his mushy brain like the crash of cannon fire. He reached out and grabbed the noisy object, recognized its shape as that of a metal bucket. And just in time, for at that moment his stomach rebelled against the spinning world and started to empty itself. He tottered up onto his knees and hung his head over the bucket. He knelt there for what seemed like an eternity, coughing and retching until he was sure his body was hollowed out and there wasn't a thing left inside him but air and pain.

He was still bent over like that when the door slammed open and bright light streamed over him. Blinking, shielding his eyes with one hand, Wager peered up and saw the old man step through the doorway, towering over him. Johnson looked angry, his gray-bearded face the visage of a wrathful god. He sniffed at the air; the foul scent of Wager's retching filled the tiny room.

"So you got sick, did you? I knew you would."

"Can't you just go away and let me die in peace?"

47

"You aren't half as dead as you're gonna be, Sam Wager."

Groaning, Wager pulled himself around to a sitting position. He held his head in his hands. It felt as if it might roll off if he didn't keep a tight grip on it. "What is it now?" he muttered.

"You're responsible, you brought death to this house. Now she's gone."

"What are you talking about?"

Johnson raised his fists. They looked as big and deadly as ball-peen hammers. "You and those bastards in town," the old man hissed. "Skelly's killers, all of you. That murderin' skunk, I should have done right by him way back when. Lord knows I've paid since then. But it ends here and now. I'll kill the whole lot of you if I have to, one by one. Starting with you. You'll pay for hurting my Sarah."

"For God's sake, talk sense. Where's Sarah? Has something happened to her?"

"Gone," Johnson said.

That single word seemed to drain all the strength from his body. His head hung low, and he shook all over like a man in the grip of a fever. Now that his eyes had cleared a bit, Wager saw the tears on the old man's cheeks.

"What do you mean?" Wager asked. "Gone where?"

"To town."

"To find Lawson and Price?" Wager's head came up. "You mean she's going after them all by herself?"

Johnson nodded. "She took my rifle."

The hair rose on the back of Wager's neck. "Dammit, man, why did you let her go? We've got to stop her!"

"Can't. She's gone," Johnson mumbled. His eyes were blank, and he muttered as if to himself. "Can't find the horses . . . can't see nothing . . . she's gone."

Wager struggled to his feet. He stood there swaying; the room wouldn't hold still, and his head felt like it was full of mush. But the acid fear in the pit of his stomach was worse. "We got to go," he said.

Johnson didn't hear him. He stared blankly at the floor, lost in a private oblivion. He didn't seem to care about killing Wager anymore. Or about anything. He just stood there and sobbed.

Wager stepped around him.

He stumbled down the corridor, clinging to the walls for support. His head clanged like a church bell, and he wanted worse than anything simply to lie back and close his eyes to the whole world. But his mind kept flashing an image of Sarah. Sarah in a wooden box, her eyes blank and cold. He took a deep breath and kept moving.

Staggering along, he emerged into the cabin's main room. By the standards of most frontier homes, it was spacious, almost palatial. There were windows on almost every wall, and even curtains. A large, colorful throw rug covered the hardwood floor, and there were furnishings in abundance, some of them crudely hand-fashioned, and others as elegant as any in a banker's New York mansion. The chairs were all different in color and design, but they all looked comfortable and well worn.

Wager's attention went immediately to the open gun cabinet. He lurched across the room. There was nothing left inside the cabinet except a shotgun, an assortment of knives, and an old black powder flintlock that looked as if it had been gathering dirt and rust since the War for Independence. Wager grabbed up the shotgun and a handful of shells. It wasn't what he would have asked for, but it would have to do.

When he turned around, Johnson was standing back in the shadows of the hallway. He was slumped against the wall, looking pale and gray, and somehow even more ancient than he was. "You really going after her?" he said.

"Somebody's got to. If we don't try, she'll end up as cold as that boy out there."

Johnson glanced up at Wager, then quickly lowered his eyes. "I'm an old man," he said. "I can't hardly see from here to where you're standing."

Johnson's voice trembled emotionally, and Wager was struck

with sympathy for the old man and his helplessness. "Don't worry. I'll bring her back to you."

Johnson nodded, but there was no hope in his voice. "You do that, Wager. All there is, anymore. She's the last."

Wager didn't understand any of that, but there was no time for explanations. He walked out onto the porch. Rain was falling, spitting on the dust, and the wind was wailing through the trees like the droning cries of a lost child. He glanced at the buckboard, frowned when he saw the empty harnesses.

"She hid the horses," Johnson said at his back. "Didn't want us following. She wants to do it all herself."

Why not? Wager thought. We all die by ourselves. But he kept the thought to himself. He bent his head to the rain and hurried across the yard to the small lean-to outbuilding that served as Johnson's barn.

The barn was empty. Wager felt like swearing, but couldn't think of a thing to say. His head ached so much that even searching through it for a proper curse was an exercise in agony. Maybe later.

Slowly he turned in a full circle, peering across the clearing at the various trails leading off into the tangled forest. She could have hidden the horses anywhere; stumbling through the brush searching for them looked like nothing more than a good way to waste valuable time. He had no idea how long he'd been unconscious, how much lead she might have on him. For all he knew, it might already be too late.

The curses started to come to his lips more easily now. For there was only one choice: he would have to go on foot.

It was about four miles to town, a long hoof but not an impossible distance. If he kept a good pace, he could make it in a little over a half-hour. Even on horseback, Sarah probably wouldn't go much faster. Her horse would shy at racing over the craggy, up-and-down scrabble paths along the mountain-sides. A man on foot, with a decent enough reason, could force himself to be less sensible.

Lightning crackled across the dark sky, and thunder boomed

in the distance, sounding exactly like gunfire. The thought of a gunshot firmed it up for Wager. His decision made, he cinched up his coat so it wouldn't flap and slow him down. Then he balanced the shotgun in one hand and pushed off down the hillside in a slow, tentative run.

His legs felt stiff as boards, and each step sent a jarring pain shooting along his spine, up to bounce around his throbbing head. After one step Wager knew he was going to die. After two steps he began praying he would.

Grimly, he pushed on, trying to mesh his breathing with his stride. He knew it would get easier. It had to. For the first few minutes he was convinced being dragged by a stampeding stallion would be easier.

He lurched along woodenly, alternately gasping and groaning. It seemed the far side of forever before he had even reached the edge of the clearing. Into the darkness of the pines, where the air seemed sweet and sticky, and the rain drumming overhead sounded like a hundred pursuers on his tail.

But once on the other side of the trees, the ground fell away and it was all downhill. Wager stumbled along, and as he neared the point where he and Sarah had first met, he gradually settled into the pace he wanted, not fast and not slow, just a steady loping gait that would eat up distance without wearing him down. It was a pace the Indians called a chase-walk, and Wager had heard of Indian hunters who could maintain it for hours, even days at a time, relentlessly stalking much faster prey until the animal finally collapsed from exhaustion.

It had been years since Wager had done any running at all, not since he was a boy galloping through the hilly woodlands of eastern Kansas. He had done his share of running back then. Any boy with a farmer-father with a long list of chores that hadn't been done knew how to run like the very devil. The feel of the stride, the breathing, the swing of the arms, it all came back to him now. It was something you never forgot.

As his blood pumped and his muscles warmed, the ache in

his head dulled a bit, and he actually began to feel better. His mind began to think clearly again. Which was a mixed blessing. Now he began to think about what he was literally running himself into.

What was he doing? What was it to him, really, if Sarah wanted to get herself killed? Surely he couldn't be attracted to her; in the short time he'd known her she had threatened him with a knife and a gun, accused him of being a child-killer, scratched up his face, spit on him, then stood by and watched the old man split open his skull. Sure, who wouldn't be attracted to a woman like that?

Now here he was, busting a gut in order to step between a wildcat girl and two gunslingers, all three of whom would gladly turn and shoot him down without a second thought. Craziness.

He was caught in the middle of an insane shooting war, and all because of a lousy hundred dollars. Greed. The very word put a sour taste in the back of his throat; every time his life took a bad turn it was because of greed. He should ask someone to cut off his fingers the next time they started grasping for money.

If he lived to see a next time.

Wager, he thought, you're crazier than any of them. At least they know what they're shooting for. Here you are, running toward your own death, and you don't even know why. Sarah and Johnson had obstinately refused to explain even the smallest detail of what it was all about. He put together all the bits and pieces that he understood about the whole squabble, and it didn't add up to what bears leave in the woods.

He knew only one thing for certain: he had to hurry or the next time he saw Sarah they would be laying her out in a six-foot hole. The thought of seeing the fire go out in those warm dark eyes disturbed him in ways he couldn't understand. He couldn't let that happen, not because of him, even if his part in it had been that of an innocent dupe.

The confusion was making his head ache again, so he shoved

it all mentally aside and tried to let his mind go blank. How hard could that be for someone like him? he thought bitterly.

He ran on recklessly, scrambling down the steep slopes, racing with abandon, pitching himself headlong, and trusting that the next step would not send him tumbling. On and on. Concentrate, just one foot in front of the other, then the next stride, and then the next. He lowered his head and pushed himself along even faster. He had to make it in time, he had to. Wager, the mighty hero, racing toward danger.

God, he was glad nobody could see him doing this.

# CHAPTER 8

SHERIDAN was a hung-over mining town that had seen its boom and glory days in 1878, and the beginning of its demise in 1879. Early 1879. The few veins of silver in the surrounding hills were quickly bought up by the all-powerful Anaconda monopoly, appraised by their geologists, and then just as quickly abandoned.

The town survived purely by virtue of its location. The place that had no gold or silver was a convenient stopping point between the settlements to the north and south that did. It was a place where everybody was coming or going. Bull trains plodded through, one day this way and the next another. The town's current prosperity could be measured by counting the oxen that stood idle on the muddy main street. The economy was—to put it kindly—flexible. The cost of a meal, a drink, or a pound of flour fluctuated in accordance with the shipping rates of the overland freight companies. Charges that could rise or fall in the time between breakfast and lunch.

Or, just as likely, between supper and the dawn. For as a roadside parasite, Sheridan was a town that never closed its doors. The lights burned all night long, and no man with money was ever turned away. The town offered two dance halls, one church, five saloons, and one vaguely churchlike building that doubled as both. The self-appointed minister of that establishment was renowned for the brevity of his sermons, the smoothness of his home brew, and the extreme loyalty of his parishioners.

Sarah rode in from the north and pulled up on a rise, pausing to survey the town sprawled out below her. She had been in Sheridan only once before, on the day she had arrived

54

to seek out Ethan Johnson. She had wandered the town for an hour before locating someone who could give her directions to Johnson's homestead. That short time had been more than enough for her. Sheridan struck her as a wild, uncivilized place, full of drunk and ill-mannered men. It was noisy and dirty and altogether a place to avoid. If she had had to stay one minute longer, she thought she would take off back to St. Louis, on foot if necessary.

She headed out into the mountains the very moment she learned the proper direction. The wildness of the open spaces was intimidating, but not nearly so much so as what she put behind her.

That had been almost a year ago. Now as she sat astride her horse and peered down at the crudely boarded buildings and the dark lines of mud that passed for streets, she wrinkled her nose in distaste. Nothing seemed to have changed.

Shaking off her hesitation, she nudged the mare in the ribs with her heels and started down the hill. Her back stiffened, and she sat tall on the horse's bare back, her face set in a frown of concentration. And if her hands on the reins trembled slightly, well, she told herself, it was only because of the cold wind and the rain that had plastered her coat to her back.

As usual, the main street was lined with wagons. A single long bull train was posed in single file, running from one edge of town to the other. The clank of oxen chains was a constant noise, a counterpoint to the never-ending music that blared from the dance halls and saloons. She could barely hear any of it over the pounding of her heart.

The few scattered buildings on the edge of town were homes of the permanent residents, separated from the racket and activity of the central businesses. All the houses looked deserted; with winter's passing, the freight lines were running more often, and no one had time for anything but attending to the needs and wants of the bull drivers. Sarah passed by the houses and did not see a single soul until she neared the center of town.

Then, as she rode by the open doors of a smithy's shop, she saw a young boy inside, laboring over a bellows. The boy saw her, too, and his mouth opened in apparent wonderment. Sarah pulled up her horse as he wandered outside, gawking up at her with a dazed expression.

"Hello," Sarah said hesitantly, made uneasy by the intensity of his interest. "Perhaps you could help me."

The boy's lips beat soundlessly for a moment, like a pump handle before the water is primed. "You . . . you're a girl, ain't you?" he suddenly blurted.

"A woman, yes."

"I don't see many girls around here wearing pants. And I ain't never seen one ridin' bareback before. Ain't you supposed to ride a sidesaddle, or something?"

"Why?"

The directness of Sarah's response took him aback. He frowned and scratched his head as if he had developed a sudden itch. Finally he shrugged. "I don't know, exactly. That's just what I heard girls did. Those that don't ride in wagons and buggies and such-like, I mean. I never thought about it much, I guess."

Sarah sighed. "Listen, I'd like to ask you something."

"To tell you the truth, I never seen a sidesaddle before. What does one look like?"

"Would you please listen? I'm looking for two men, strangers in town named Lawson and Price. They're big fellows, wear fancy clothes; they probably came in a day or two ago. Do you know them?"

The boy nodded. "Seen 'em once." He jerked a thumb over his shoulder back toward the blacksmith shop. "Lew put up their horses when they came to town. Yesterday it was."

"Do you know where I could find them now?"

The boy's hand moved from scratching his head to scratching his chin without missing a beat. "Lemme see. . . . Yeah, I heard one of 'em tell Lew they was taking rooms in the hotel. And if they ain't there, well, there's about five or so places they could be." He scratched faster as another thought occurred to him. "That's right, this is the afternoon the preacher writes his sermons . . . so yeah, there's just five."

Sarah didn't understand, and didn't care. "What places?" she said impatiently.

"Saloons," the boy said, honestly surprised by the question. "Where else? Say, you ain't planning to go in them places to look for them yourself, are you?"

"Why not?" Sarah said defiantly.

"You'll cause one heck of a stir, that's why. I don't think none of the men around here have seen a girl as pretty as you in a long, long time." He lowered his eyes shyly. "I know I ain't."

Sarah smiled down at the boy. Perhaps he had a point. The appearance of a new woman in town, especially one dressed as she was and toting a rifle, might create more of a disturbance than she wanted to deal with. "No, I don't think I will," she said. She slung her leg over the horse's back and slid down to the ground. "Maybe you'd go find them for me. Would you do that?"

"Me? Well, I don't know." The boy peered back inside the smithy shop. "I'm supposed to be working for Lew right now."

"I'll pay you a dollar."

"Yeah?" The boy's eyes lit up. He didn't have to scratch long before coming to a decision. "All right, I guess it won't take all that long. Sure, I'll do it."

Sarah fished in her coat and came out with a gold coin. It was her last, the end of the money she had brought west with her. She handed it over without hesitation.

The boy's eyes shone like the well-rubbed coin. "Yes, ma'am. What am I supposed to tell them when I find 'em?"

"Say that Sarah Martin wants to see them. Make sure you get the name right, Sarah Martin. Tell them I'll be waiting outside the hotel."

"That's all I tell 'em?"

"That will be plenty," Sarah said.

The boy decided to skip the hotel and start directly on the saloons. His logic proved right, and he came upon Lawson and Price in the second place he checked. There was no doubt these were the men he wanted; he knew everyone in town, and nearly all the bull drivers. One thing was for sure—these men weren't bull drivers.

Ben Lawson sat at a table, idly flipping through a deck of cards. He dealt first from the top of the deck, then the bottom, then the middle, all with an easy, casual motion too quick for the eye to follow. It was something he liked to play at to keep his dexterity sharp. Tom Price sat across the table, watching the cards drop and every few minutes tipping back his head in a loud yawn. He had seen Lawson's card tricks many times before. Lawson said the cards helped keep his gun hand quick, but Price didn't see how guns and cards had much to do with each other. He was content to sit there and guzzle beer. Every now and then, he would glance up the staircase where he had seen two saloon girls disappear with a couple of miners. The women had been sort of old, and more than a little rough looking, but Price didn't figure that would bother him. In a dung-heap town like this, they probably came cheap.

He frowned when he was glancing that way again and a young boy stepped up, blocking his view. "You want something, kid?" Price growled.

"You Ben Lawson?" the boy asked nervously. He had one hand stuck in his pocket as if clutching something important. The other hand scratched a furrow across his tangled hair.

"That's me," Lawson said without looking up from his cards. "What do you want, boy?"

"I'm s'posed to . . . I got a message to give you."

Lawson tilted his head back with a bored look. "I've seen you before, down to the stables. What happened, did that friggin' smithy do something to my horse?"

"No, sir. The message ain't from him."

"Out with it, boy. Hurry up," Price grumbled. The girls had

reappeared at the top of the staircase, and he leaned around the kid for a closer look.

"Okay." The boy took a deep breath. "I'm to tell you . . . there's a girl named Sarah Martin wants to see you."

"What?" Both men sat bolt upright in their chairs. "What'd you say?"

The boy paled. "Sarah Martin. That's what she said. She told me to say she'll be waiting outside the hotel."

Lawson pushed the cards together in a neat stack. "What's this Sarah Martin look like?"

"Pretty, real pretty."

"Small woman, dark hair cut real short?"

"Yessir, that's the one."

"She alone?" Price asked.

The boy shrugged. "I guess so. I didn't see no one else."

"When did you see her?"

"Just a minute ago. She came riding by the stable and asked me if I knew where to find two strangers what was in town. You, I mean."

Lawson rocked his chair back on the hind legs. "She was on horseback, huh? Did she come in from the north?"

"I think so." The boy scratched briefly. "Riding bareback, without a saddle or even a harness or nothing."

Lawson and Price exchanged a look. "You're sure you didn't see anyone else with her—like maybe an old man, big guy with gray hair and a beard?"

"You mean Wolfer Johnson?" the boy asked.

Lawson's chair plunked flat on the floor. "What makes you think I'm talking about Johnson?" he said in a low voice.

"It was his horse she was riding."

"What makes you so sure of that?"

"I know all the horses 'round here," the boy said, " 'cause we tend to 'em down at the stables. We ain't never kept Mr. Johnson's horse, but I noticed him once or twice, the times he's come to town. It pays to know your customers, Lew says."

Price smiled. Lawson smiled. The boy looked at them both, then smiled. Hesitantly.

Price shook his head. "So the old man sent the girl to do his fighting for him. Can you believe it?"

Lawson gave his partner a stern look. Price shut his mouth quickly.

Lawson turned to the boy. "Lew was right. 'Cause you knew your customers, you get this." He handed over a gold coin.

"Thank you, sir," the boy said quietly. He didn't act as excited as when Sarah had paid him. It wasn't clear in his head, but he had a growing sense that maybe he'd done something wrong.

"Get back to your horses now, son." The boy needed no coaxing. He took off without so much as a glance back.

Price leaned across the table once they were alone. "How's it sound to you? You think maybe it's a trap?"

Lawson pushed back his coattails and rested his hand on the butt of his revolver. As his hand settled, he smiled. "It will be," he said. "But not for us."

# CHAPTER 9

SARAH stood in the shade under the hotel awning and glanced down the street one way, then quickly down the other. She had been doing that for several minutes, and her neck muscles felt like tightly strung barbed wire. Every once in a while she would catch herself and realize she was holding her breath. Got to stay calm. She gripped the rifle tight against her leg so it wouldn't show too much, and pressed her back against the wall of the hotel. Her free hand beat out a nervous rhythm on the rough boards behind her.

There was plenty of activity to watch. The bull train was moving out now, and dozens of bleary-eyed men were stumbling out of the saloons. They moved listlessly up and down the long line of wagons, searching for their own rigs. Most of them were drunk; those who weren't seemed sorry about the fact. Though they weren't dressed alike, they all wore the same uniform of mud and dust from the miles they'd already traveled. A visit to the bathhouse apparently hadn't been high on their list of things to do during their brief stop. The things they had to say about the leadman who had summoned them back to work weren't any cleaner.

Still no sign of the two gunmen. Sarah craned her neck to the right yet once more, then almost jumped out of her skin as a hand dropped onto her blind-side shoulder. She spun around; staring back at her, point-blank, was a pair of leering bloodshot eyes.

"Whoa, little lady!" the man cackled. "Didn't mean to scare you none. This is just harmless ol' Jack Harper here is all." He twisted his lips into a grin, revealing teeth like the niblets on an ear of bug-spoiled corn.

61

"What do you want?" Sarah demanded.

"Why, just to meet you is all." The man tightened his grip on her shoulder. "Where you been hiding yourself, girl? I know for sure I ain't seen nothing like you around here before. And I surely would know, because I been alookin'."

Sarah took a deep breath. She immediately regretted it. The smell of him was nauseating. The true color of his shirt showed through only in the damp patches where sweat had washed away the layers of dust. He swayed drunkenly, falling against her. Sarah shuddered.

"Take your hand off me, please."

"Aww, what's the matter, honey? I'm just trying to be friendly." He took his hand from her shoulder, but then planted it against the wall, supporting himself as he leaned over her. "Whattaya say, how about you and me go have some fun together, eh? Don't you worry, I'll pay whatever it's worth. They all says ol' Jack Harper, he's generous to a fault."

Sarah stiffened. She turned slowly and looked him straight in the eyes. "You stink, mister. And your breath would make a buzzard wince."

"You got a sense of humor. Good, I like that."

Sarah motioned to the bull train, which was slowly starting to move down the street. "You belong with them?" she asked.

He grinned smugly. "Yeah. But don't let it worry your pretty little head, honey. I can always catch up to them later."

Sarah brought the rifle up and placed the muzzle firmly against his upper lip. "You'd best catch up to them *now*."

"Jesus!" The man's eyes bulged. "You're crazy, lady! What do you think you're doin'?"

"Shut up and get moving. Before I freshen your breath by letting some air in."

He got the idea. The man stumbled over his own legs in his haste and tumbled to the sidewalk with a loud crash. Glancing up at her fearfully, he scrambled to his feet and ran for the bull train as if a pack of wolves were nipping at his heels.

A loud chorus of laughter arose from the men on the passing wagons.

"Way to go, girl!"

"Ol' Jack's eyes always were bigger than his . . . uh, stomach!"

Some of the men waved at Sarah; one or two even clapped. She sagged back against the wall, feeling flushed from relief and the sudden attention. It seemed everyone in the street was looking at her. She lowered her head, feeling her cheeks redden.

Then as the commotion died down, there came the hollow sound of a single man clapping his hands. Sarah looked up and saw him step away from the crowd. A black-bearded man in finely cut clothes.

"You handled that freight hauler very well," Ben Lawson said. "But it doesn't come as a surprise to me. I always told Tom there's a lot of fire in that little woman."

Sarah locked eyes with the gunman. It wasn't fire she felt within her, but a numbing chill. "Oh? And where might that murdering partner of yours be right now?" she asked.

Lawson pointed back the way he had come. "Inside the saloon, passed out cold, and snoring loud enough to wake a bear in the dead of winter." He smiled. "He'll be real sorry he missed you."

"Sure. And you were just too kindhearted to wake him when you got my message."

"I didn't see the point of bothering him." Lawson's smile was cold, mocking. "We can have a little talk together, just you and me, can't we?"

Sarah felt a bead of sweat run along her eyebrow. "What I came here for has little to do with talking," she said.

"Yeah, is that so?" Lawson's eyes shifted briefly to the men gathered around them. A small crowd was forming, men watching curiously, aroused by the odd tone of their voices. The gunman settled his gaze back on her and said smoothly, "Well, then, just what did you come here to do?"

"To put you and Price in your graves."

A murmur rippled through the crowd like the buzzing from a nest of hornets. Some stepped back, but most stayed where they were, not yet believing.

"I don't want to fight you," Lawson said. "I don't go around shooting women."

"No, just little boys!" Sarah spat. "You didn't have any qualms about killing Tommy, did you?"

"I don't know any Tommy."

Sarah stepped up to the edge of the sidewalk. "He was only five years old, and you killed him! You shot him and stuffed him and threw him in a box like he was nothing but trash to be hauled off somewhere and dumped."

"*Stuffed* him?" Lawson said derisively, loud enough for the crowd to hear. Then he lowered his voice to a gentle, soothing tone. "Lady, that's crazy talk. I don't know who this Tommy is or why you've decided to pick on me. But I'm not going to get mad. I know you can't help yourself. Something in your head's just not right."

There was a hum of agreement from the crowd. In the back of her mind Sarah realized what he was doing, how he was playing on the crowd's sympathy, getting them on his side. But she was too far gone to care.

"You are scum, Lawson," Sarah whispered. She levered a cartridge into the Winchester's chamber. "I'm going to put this bullet right in your head, exactly where you shot Tommy."

"Now, calm down," Lawson said, as if talking to a child. "Why don't you just put that gun away for a minute and we can talk about it nice and peaceful."

"We've talked enough."

Lawson shrugged for the crowd's benefit and held his hands out to his sides. "Don't do this; don't make me shoot you."

"You aren't going to shoot anybody, you bastard. Never again. You're just going to be dead."

Lawson sighed fairly convincingly. Only someone listening very closely could have detected the muted tone of satisfaction in his voice. "If that's the way you're determined to have it, lady. You don't leave me any choice. I don't want to draw on you. But I'm sure not going to die to please some crazy woman's delusions."

The crowd fell back, scattering to get out of the way. No one made a sound. The freight wagons were still going past. In the hushed silence their movements sounded unnaturally loud: the groaning of the weighted wagons, the plodding steps of the oxen, and still the clanking of the chains, a strangely ominous noise, like the rattle of death in a man's throat.

Lawson spoke very softly. "All right," he said. "Come ahead, girl."

Sarah felt as if her whole body were made of ice. She knew if she moved she would shatter into a thousand brittle pieces. But she had to move, had to see it through. Death would be no worse than seeing this smug killer go free.

"Well? Changed your mind, girl?"

"I'm ready," Sarah said quietly.

# CHAPTER 10

WAGER tripped over a stone and staggered drunkenly for a few yards before righting himself. He wondered longingly if he could just throw himself down and roll down the hill into town. He knew he couldn't run another step without dying right in his tracks. Actually, it didn't sound that bad; at least dead men get to lie still. His ribs felt as if he had been split wide open and stitched back together with a long, dull needle; his feet were slipping and rubbing inside his sweaty-slimy boots, and he knew they were just a hair's breadth from bursting into flame.

Chase-walk? Dumb Indians, he thought. No wonder the whites had defeated them. If they had really hunted this way, they must have been too tired to fight.

The last hill, the town in sight. He tried to raise his head and look over the streets while he was still high enough for an overview. As soon as he did, he missed his footing, and new muscles joined in the dance of pain. He gave it up. It was all he could do to keep watching the ground and forcing himself on, one plodding step after another.

He didn't realize he had made it until the shadow of a building fell across him. He glanced up and saw buildings on both sides of him. It was like seeing the skies open up and a smiling god beckon him into heaven. He let his rubbery legs stop, moaning in relief and utter joy.

So much for the easy part.

Now all he had to do was stop a gunfight. Of course, first he had to find it. That proved to be no problem, however. He had gone up the street only a little ways, shuffling alongside a line of departing freight wagons, when he saw the crowd gathered outside the hotel. He had no doubt at all whom he would find in the center of that crowd.

Another bull wagon passed by him. On impulse, Wager grabbed at the frame and hoisted himself up in the back end. He glanced inside the canvas-covered bed and flinched; there was already a man inside there. The man seemed equally surprised to find Wager hanging on the wagon and peering in at him. He was flopped out on a stack of feed sacks, looking like something the cats dragged in. Dragged a long way. There were two empty bottles beside him, and his eyes rolled as if he were seeing two of everything, but neither too clearly.

He squinted at Wager, focused on the shotgun in his hand, then let his head fall back with a groan. "Oh, thank God. Someone has come to do the decent thing. Go ahead, shoot me quick and put me outta my misery."

Wager smiled. "Sorry. I'm saving these shells for someone else."

"Lucky bastard," the man said. Then he turned his head and started to be sick all over himself. Wager turned away.

The wagon was carrying him closer and closer to the commotion outside the hotel. From atop the wagon bed, he could see over the crowd. What he saw made his heart start pounding like a drum. It was Sarah, with the rifle at her side, and Lawson, with his hand hovering near his holstered revolver. Clearly they were not having a friendly chat about the weather. He heard Lawson's growl clearly. "Well? Changed your mind, girl?"

"I'm ready," Sarah said in a small voice.

Even from there, Wager could see how she trembled, her body rocking back and forth like a sapling in a gusting wind. But she stood her ground, determined to see it through.

Frantically, Wager climbed higher on the wagon, peering over the canvas cover to scan both sides of the street. He was upset by what he could not see—namely, a gunman named Tom Price.

"Okay, I'll make it easy for you," Lawson said. "And fair for the both of us. I'll count slowly, loud and clear. Go for it on the count of three."

Wager didn't hear if Sarah replied. For at that moment he spotted a shadowy movement inside the hotel, someone just on the other side of the large window. A second later the hotel door swung open a mere crack.

"One," Lawson rumbled.

Wager's skin prickled as he caught a glimpse of sunlight slanting off blued steel. A gun barrel nosed out the crack in the hotel doorway.

The bull wagon had almost come abreast of the street fight. Without hesitation, Wager leaped down and plunged headlong into the crowd.

"Two."

Wildly, Wager fought his way forward, shoving men from his path left and right. "Let me through, outta the way, dammit!" He broke out on the other side just at the final second.

"Three."

Wager screamed, "Sarah!"

With a speed born of desperation, he leaped into the open ten feet from the hotel door, loosing both barrels. The shotgun bucked in his hands, booming like peals of fatal thunder.

The shots took Sarah and Lawson by surprise. Diverted, they both turned, forgetting each other for the moment. Sarah stood rooted by confusion, stunned by the sensations that assaulted her. The next few seconds played out before her like a terrible dream, something she could only experience, not affect or change.

The hotel door had been adorned with a window of stained glass, a design intricately woven in a kaleidoscope of colors. Sarah saw it suddenly dissolve into a thousand pieces. Splinters of glass flew everywhere, falling in a deadly rain with an absurdly delicate tinkling and popping noise.

The hotel door crashed open. A man stood there posed in the doorway, swaying on unsteady legs. Blood spouted from his body in a dozen places; his face was shredded like torn cloth. Embedded slivers of glass sparkled from his flesh, catching the sunlight like fallen teardrops.

Sarah's breath caught in her throat. Disfigured though it was, it was a face she knew.

Dazed, she watched Tom Price lurch away from the door. He took a few shaky steps, then stopped, staring directly at her. His eyes made Sarah's skin crawl—the pain in them, the sorrowful anguish. She was stunned to witness something so human in this monster she had hated for so long. She tried to look away, but she could not.

Tom Price spoke to her, pointing an accusing finger. "You . . . killed me," he said, as if the idea were a surprise to them both. Then the legs went soft beneath him and he collapsed, dropping like a scarecrow suddenly stripped of its supporting pole. His body settled with sudden quietness. Mesmerized, Sarah watched the gun drop from his hand, skitter across the sidewalk, and tumble into the mud.

Almost in the same instant, it seemed, her eyes went to the other man. Smoke was still rising from the shotgun in his hands. He turned, and with a start she realized it was Sam Wager. His image stunned her; it made no sense. It was too much, too fast; she could not understand how he was there, what he had done. Nor did she understand the look on his face as he met her eyes. An imploring look, almost pleading.

So slowly the pieces came together in her mind. Too late, she remembered the other gunman. She jerked her eyes back and saw Lawson diverting his aim, the gun in his hand swinging to bear on Sam Wager.

Wager was already moving. Dropping the spent shotgun, he dove for Price's fallen revolver. But it was hopeless.

Lawson's gun roared, picking Wager out of midair. Wager was hurled aside as if struck by a giant hand. Thudding to the ground, he tumbled over twice and fetched up hard against the edge of the sidewalk. As he came to rest, his hand dropped to clutch at his ribs. A bright red stain appeared beneath his fumbling fingers.

"You worthless, trouble-making bastard," Lawson growled. His voice was so low it sounded like a distant echo of the gun report. He turned his back on Sarah, fully ignoring her. Slowly and precisely, he raised his gun at arm's length and sighted down the barrel at Wager's head.

Sarah screamed, "No!" Finally shaking off her daze, she hastily swung her rifle, jerked back the trigger.

The slug took Lawson in the back of the thigh, kicked the leg out from under him. The gunman fell back like a toppled tree. He groaned as he tumbled, but the grip on his gun stayed firm. Rolling over, he looked up at Sarah and bared his teeth. "You bitch. For that you die. Nobody takes me down."

Sarah saw the gun swing toward her. Frantically, she pulled back on the trigger again. Nothing. In her panic she had forgotten to eject the spent shell. Desperate now, she fought the heavy lever action of the Winchester. She saw Lawson grin over the sights of his revolver. There was no time left.

Then, just as Lawson squeezed off his shot, a boot swung solidly against his wrist, kicking the hand upward so that the bullet soared up to wound the clouds.

"What the hell . . . ?" Lawson glared up at the man standing over him. He started to pull his gun around, but the boot came down on the wrist again, pinned it to the earth, and ground on the joint until Lawson's eyes narrowed in pain.

"Leave it go, mister. 'Less you want me to break that hand."

Lawson spat, "This ain't your fight. Clear the hell out of it."

"We don't shoot women around here, mister. Gives the town a bad name." The man was heavyset, dressed in a sheepskin coat and a precisely blocked Stetson. His broad face smiled. "Not that we got much to brag about, as it is. Now, what is this all about?"

"None of your damned business!"

The man calmly pushed his coat open, revealing a silver star pinned to his shirt. "I'm sayin' this badge makes it my business.

Let me introduce myself: I'm Cal Fuller—Sheriff Fuller to you. I have a feeling we're going to get downright well acquainted, you and I. . . . "

A loud, dry click at his back took the sheriff's attention. Sarah had finally succeeded in ejecting the rifle shell. With a small cry of triumph, she started forward.

At a motion from Fuller, two men grabbed Sarah from behind. One pinned her arms while the other twisted the rifle from her hands.

"No, no. You can't!" Sarah bucked in the man's arms, kicking and fighting like a wild horse. Fuller squinted in a look of amusement. Others stared at her with awe, perhaps fear. For there was genuine madness in her eyes now. She screamed and screamed, a raw, ugly sound, wrenched from the gut. "Shoot him, kill him now! Let me go, you don't understand . . . you got to—you must let me kill him!"

The sheriff frowned at her and shook his head. "Now, you quiet down and don't give me any more trouble. Nobody's going to kill anybody, you hear? You just quiet down or I'll lock you away where you can't bother nobody, and let you scream your crazy head off."

Sarah burst into frustrated tears. "You just don't understand."

Fuller pushed back his Stetson and sighed. "Well, you're right enough there. And I don't suppose we're getting any-place by standing around here." He jerked a finger at some men in the crowd. "You there, come pitch in. We got to clear all this mess up. Drag the bodies down to the undertaker's while I take these two somewhere we can talk."

A man standing over Wager called out, "This one, too, Sheriff?"

"Why not? He's dead, ain't he?"

"I think he's still breathing."

Sarah broke a hand free and grabbed at the sheriff's arm. "You can't waste time talking about him. You got to get him to a doctor."

"I thought I told you to be quiet, girl."

"Dammit, you can't let him die. Wager, he . . . he saved my life."

"Wager, you say?" Fuller turned and squinted. "Damn, is that Sam Wager? I didn't even notice."

"Yes. Help him, please."

Fuller sighed. "Well, hell." He stabbed a finger at two more men. "Grab up that man and haul him over to Doc Court's place, real quicklike. But you be careful with him, or I'll bury my boot up both your backsides."

"Thank you, Sheriff," Sarah said softly.

Fuller shook her hand off his arm. "Don't go getting the wrong idea, girl. That no-good borrowed ten dollars off me last week. Nobody dies owing me money, not if I got something to say about it. He ain't gonna get off that easy."

# CHAPTER 11

WAGER came awake with a sudden start and a nagging sense of apprehension, like the holdover from a bad dream. A harsh white light was blazing in his eyes. Through the haze he could dimly make out a young male face peering back at him with an oddly intense curiosity.

"What are you looking at?" Wager asked. The weakness of his own voice surprised him.

"Your pupils look pretty good," the man said.

"That's nice. My what?"

"Your eyes, Mr. Wager."

"I never had a man tell me I had nice eyes before."

The light was pulled away, and Wager saw the man smile. "Perhaps I should tell you who I am."

"Sure."

"Michael Court's my name, Mr. Wager. *Doctor* Michael Court."

Wager blinked. The man had a mustache as black as night; it hung down completely covering his lips, and the ends nearly touched his jaw. But even with all that hair on his face, he didn't look more than fifteen years old.

Court frowned. "Don't say it. I know—I look too young to be a doctor, right? Everybody thinks that. But rest assured, I'm qualified and licensed, and experienced. Don't let the face fool you."

"No. I was just going to ask what am I doing here with a doctor?"

"You were shot, Mr. Wager."

"Oh, yeah." Images of the gunfight came back to him now, but they seemed remote, unreal.

73

"You're a very lucky man," Court said. "The bullet missed your heart by only a couple of inches."

"A lucky man it would have missed altogether."

Court smiled. "True. You do have a very serious wound."

"How come I don't hurt, then?" Wager sat up a little, experimentally. A spasm of pain shot along his rib cage. His lips tightened. "Uh, forget that question."

Court gently pushed him back down. "You're in shock. That's why you don't feel as much pain as you might expect. But don't let it fool you; you're gravely injured, and it's important you don't move around."

"Should I be scared, Doc?"

"What you should be is quiet. Lie still now while I finish the examination."

Wager did as he was told. While the doctor bent over the wound in his side, Wager took the opportunity to look around. The room was fairly good-sized, but it looked small because every available inch was taken up with shelves and cabinets and counters. The shelves went right up to the ceiling. On the ones to his right sat glass jars containing a pale liquid in which floated odd bits of matter that looked like raw meat. Wager was able to recognize a brain and a liver and such when he saw one. There were plenty of both organs in the jars, though the sizes and appearances differed a bit from the ones he remembered having seen at slaughtering time when he was a boy.

On his other side was a counter covered with an assortment of the smallest, shiniest knives Wager had ever seen. Next to that was a huge tub, emitting fumes that smelled vaguely like lye. In the corner was a rolltop desk heaped with stacks of papers, some piled neatly, others in wadded, leaning mounds. In the only clear space on the desk sat a plate containing the remains of a half-eaten meal. It, too, was leaning, toward the moldy side.

Everywhere else there were books, more books than Wager had ever seen in one place in his entire life. Books stacked neatly on the shelves, books tossed carelessly on the tabletops, books left open with dog-eared pages, and still others lying print face down. They were all thick, heavy-looking volumes, too, not at all like the slim ones Wager remembered struggling through during those long winters in the tiny Fort Scott schoolhouse.

"Why would anyone want so many books?" Wager wondered aloud. Court was busy at the other end of the room; if he heard, he didn't bother to reply. Wager felt genuinely mystified; there must have been more words in that room than any man could hope to read in a whole lifetime, he thought. Just the idea of all that reading made his head swim.

Dr. Court reappeared at his side. "Well, I think it's time we get started," he said.

"Start what?"

"You surely don't want to walk around the rest of your life with a bullet next to your heart, Mr. Wager. It has to come out."

"Are we talking about you doing an operation? On me?"

"You seem like a logical choice, yes."

"As in you take a knife and slice me open?"

Court smiled. "Unless you had someone else in mind to do it."

"Thanks, anyway. Maybe some other time."

"Don't be stupid, Mr. Wager."

"Why not? I've had plenty of practice lately." Wager waved a hand in a dismissive gesture. "Just let me lie here and rest a bit. In a few minutes I'll clear out."

Court frowned thoughtfully. "Do you mind if I show you something?" he asked.

"Sure, go ahead."

The doctor ran a finger along Wager's rib cage, delicately searching for a particular spot. He found it and applied gentle pressure.

"Hey!" Wager gasped. The pain was like a fist in the stomach.

"Do you get the idea?" Court said severely. "That's not

going to go away by itself. The bullet is lodged against the bone. That is, most of it is. There could well be fragments scattered in other places. Every time you move, you run a chance of shifting it and causing internal damage. A very simple action could cause a hemorrhage and make you bleed to death. I can't let you run that risk."

"You have a very convincing manner, Doctor."

The tension left Court's face, and his boyish smile radiated pleasure. "All right, so no more arguments. The sooner we get started, the better."

Wager sighed. "Sure." He watched Court as the young man went about gathering the articles and instruments for the operation. "Tell me, something's been bothering me, Doc. How come I've never seen you before?"

Court looked up from his table of knives. "I don't gamble and I don't drink."

"Oh," Wager said. "That would explain it all right."

Court came back to his side, smiled down at him. "I'm nearly finished with my preparations. Now it's time to get you ready."

"What do you need from me?"

Court opened a drawer in the rolltop and pulled out a tall, elegantly labeled whiskey bottle. Wager's eyes opened wide in appreciation. It was Murphy's Double Black, imported from Ireland, a single-malt renowned as the finest and most expensive whiskey in the world. He had heard about the stuff for years, but had never known anyone rich enough to have actually sipped any. Until now he had tended to believe it was just a dipso fantasy, something everyone wanted to believe in, merely because it sounded so good. The brewery at the end of the rainbow.

Court came back over and held up the bottle.

"I thought you said you don't drink."

"I don't," Court replied. "That's one reason I can afford this. I keep it only for very special purposes. There are better means of anesthesia, but they're not available here, if you know what I mean. It's one hazard of a frontier practice."

"An est-ta-who?" Wager said.

Court pushed the bottle into Wager's hand. "I want you to drink this," he said. "Just as much as you possibly can."

Wager hesitated just a second, his eyes gleaming. "Well, okay. You're the doctor."

The first belt stripped the lining from Wager's throat, sucked all the air from the room, and put tears in his eyes the size of silver dollars.

"I thought this stuff was supposed to be smooth," he gasped. "Straight varnish is smoother than this."

"It will get better," Court promised. "Just keep drinking."

Sixty-five minutes later, Wager was out cold. He had stopped his complaining long before the moment he passed out.

The bullet had flattened against one of Wager's ribs. Luckily, its head had not fragmented. It was a relatively simple procedure for Court to remove the bullet. Then he packed the wound with his own concoction of powders, doused it with alcohol, and stitched it closed. His patient slept on peacefully.

Two men were sitting out on the porch, kicked back in their chairs, smoking and watching the sunset. Court opened the door and ushered them inside. The three of them lifted Wager off the table and onto a makeshift stretcher.

"I checked around like you asked, Doc," one of the men said. "He's got a room upstairs at the Little Shanghai. That where you want we should take him?"

"That will be fine," Court said. He handed each of the men two dollars. "Thanks for your help."

"Sure, Doc. Anything else we can do for you?"

"Well, maybe there is," Court said. He handed one man the empty whiskey bottle. "Since you're going that way, could you drop in and have Kelly fill this up for me? That cheap skullbuster he makes overnight. Kelly knows what I want."

The two men picked up the stretcher clumsily and nearly tipped Wager onto the floor. He slept on, oblivious to everything. "He sure is peaceful, ain't he?" one man observed. "You sure must be a damned good surgeon, Doc." Court smiled. "I have my ways," he said.

# CHAPTER 12

THE door opened softly. Sheriff Fuller looked up from the letter he was writing. The wind came in through the open door and rustled his papers; he turned them over and set the cold coffee pot on them to hold them down. "Something I can do for you?" he asked the two men. More strangers, this seemed to be the day for them.

"Perhaps there is, Sheriff," the first man said. He was big, well over six feet and running to fat, though the elegant cut of his clothes did much to disguise that fact. "Indeed, there may be something we can do for each other."

"You could start by closing that door."

The big man nodded toward his friend. He padded softly over and pulled the door shut. This second man was almost the opposite of the other—small, dark, and whipcord lean. He moved with a stealthy grace and made barely a sound.

"Pull up some chairs," Fuller said. He rocked back and put his boots up on the edge of his desk, crossed his hands behind his head. When the two men were settled, he said, "Now, why don't you just say what you come to say?"

The big man smiled. It looked like an expression he wore easily and often. "You are direct, Sheriff. I like that in the people I do business with."

"Yeah? What kinda business you do?"

"Let me introduce ourselves. I am Vincent Skelly, from Bozeman. Does the name mean anything to you, Sheriff?"

"Can't say as it does."

"Well, no matter." The smile stayed firmly in place. He motioned toward the small, dark man. "This is my associate, John Nevers. We have come to your town on a matter of some urgency. Now, some difficulties have arisen . . . minor difficulties, I'm sure, and we require your assistance to smooth them over."

Fuller sighed and stuck a toothpick into his mouth. "You can talk plainer than that."

Skelly nodded and leaned forward in his chair, brushing at a piece of lint on his trousers. "Yes, let me come straight to the point. You have two people in your jail here, I believe, a man and a woman. I would like you to release them."

Fuller scowled. "Why would I want to do that?"

Skelly brushed the question aside. "Mr. Lawson is a business associate of mine. May I ask how he is doing?"

"He's all right."

"I understand that he was wounded in the altercation this afternoon."

"Yeah, the girl shot him," Fuller said. "Bullet went clean through his leg, though. The doc hardly spent any time with him. He's fine. Do you want to see him?"

The big man shook his head. "That won't be necessary. I heard that there was another man involved, someone named Wager. Is he here also?"

"No, he's in his room over the Shanghai."

"Is it customary for you to keep prisoners in a saloon, Sheriff? Why haven't you taken him into custody?"

"That associate of yours put a bullet two inches from his heart and damned near killed him. The doc had to operate and take it out to keep him from bleedin' to death. He's not going anywhere."

"I see," Skelly said. "And the girl? How is she?"

Fuller frowned and worked the toothpick across his mouth to the other side. "How she is is a pain. Keeps hollering for me to let her go see Wager."

"And what have you learned from her about the reasons for the altercation?"

"Not a damned thing. About that she's as tight-lipped as a two-dollar whore. Matter of fact, that Lawson fella ain't talking much either. Between the two of 'em, I know as much about that gunfight as I do about sheep shearing—and that's nothing."

Skelly and Nevers looked at each other briefly. Then Skelly turned back to Fuller. "Now, Sheriff, let me ask you one more—"

Fuller slammed his boots to the floor. "Look here, Mr. Skelly. I'd love to keep talking with you all night, but I got things to do, and to tell you the truth, I don't see where any of this is really your business. Now, if there's a point to all these questions, get to it."

Skelly's smile faded. "Very well, Sheriff. I have a proposition to make to you. First, I would like my associate released. The girl as well. A female martyr serves no one's best interests. And after all, what reason do you have to hold them? Other than a minor disturbance of the peace, no harm was done this afternoon."

"A man named Tom Price got himself dead. He might beg to differ with you on that."

"And the man who killed him was gravely wounded as well," Skelly said smoothly. "You see no problem in letting him stay in his own room. And the girl wishes to see him—well, why don't you let her? Let her stay and watch over him. Surely it won't be difficult to keep her under some form of house arrest there. Yes, that is the perfect solution. It will keep her quiet and out of the way, but she will still be available if you decide at some point in the future that you wish to arrest her again."

Fuller wavered. "Yeah, I suppose I could do that. It would get her out of my hair."

Skelly beamed and spread his hands wide apart. "You see? Your problems are solved."

"But I don't know about letting Lawson go free," Fuller said. "That won't look right."

Skelly's smile flashed on again. "You can release him into my custody, Sheriff. I will personally guarantee his good behavior, and that he will be available to you at any time."

"Yeah? And just how do I know your guarantee is good?"

Skelly dug into his pocket and produced a fat wad of bills. He began flipping through them, revealing the denominations. There was nothing smaller than a fifty. "Why don't you decide what will put your mind at ease, Sheriff? I'm sure that you can be made to see my side of this."

Fuller gulped, the toothpick dangling from his open lips. "Could be. Those are awful good-looking reasons."

# CHAPTER 13

THE morning sun crept through the window with the stealth of a burglar. Ever so slowly, the ray of light moved across the room, crawled on the bed, and eased up to touch the face of the man sleeping.

Wager opened his eyes, blinked, and let out a groan. He yanked the blanket up over his face.

"Mr. Wager?"

Beneath the covers, Wager opened his eyes in a startled reflex. "Who's out there?" he asked, his voice muffled by the blanket over his face.

"Sarah Martin, Mr. Wager." There was a pause in which he heard her moving closer to the bed. Then her voice again, soft, concerned. "Are you all right?"

Wager's arm emerged from under the blanket. His finger pointed to the window, shook up and down. Smiling, Sarah went over and drew a curtain across the window so that only a narrow shaft of light entered the room and fell well short of the bed. "All right, you can come up now," she said, barely disguising the amusement in her voice.

Like a scout sneaking up on the enemy camp, Wager cautiously eased his head out above the edge of the blanket. In the dim light he watched Sarah's silhouette move back across the room. She pulled a chair up beside the bed and sat down. The chair squeaked as it settled under her weight. The noise set off a fireworks display inside Wager's skull. He groaned.

"What's the matter?" Sarah asked.

"Do you see my head anyplace? I think it just rolled under the bed."

"Dr. Court said you would have a headache when you woke up."

"I want to know how the buffalo that trampled me got up the stairs."

Sarah picked up a mug from the nightstand, then leaned over him. "Here, he mixed up a potion for you. He said it would make you feel better."

"What's in it?"

"He said not to tell you."

Wager waved at her to take it away. "Nope, not on your life."

"It might help."

"It might kill me. I'm not touching anything made up by that medicine-show quack."

Sarah frowned at him as she put the mug back on the nightstand. "That's no way to talk about Dr. Court. He saved your life." She fell silent, and Wager felt the weight of her gaze on him. Then she added, "Just like you saved mine."

"Don't mention it," he said. "We all do foolish things, one time or another."

She said softly, "I don't think you really mean that."

Wager stared up at the ceiling. He found that if he focused on one tiny spot, and didn't blink or breathe, the pain was almost bearable.

"I've been wondering why you did it," Sarah said. "Why you risked your own life to help me."

"Me, too."

Sarah lowered her head, her voice hesitant. "I've been in trouble a long time. You're the first person who ever stood up to help me, to act like you cared. And after the way Ethan and I treated you, too. I feel so awful about that now."

"Good," Wager said grouchily. She was distracting him, and his spot on the ceiling wouldn't hold still.

She went on as if she hadn't heard. "And despite all that, you risked your life for me. I don't understand that. I'm grateful, but I'm still just . . . shocked. Thank God you're going to be all right. I don't know what I would have done if they'd killed you."

"Yeah, I'm so glad for you." A soft noise startled him, and he glanced over at her. Her eyes looked huge and warm and moist. "Are you crying?"

"What if I am?" she snapped.

"Well, nothing," he muttered, confused. "But why?"

She came to her feet abruptly, turned away so that her back was to him. Her shoulders were heaving. "Oh, how the hell should I know?" she muttered. "Do you think I have all the answers to everything, any more than you?"

Wager felt a tightness in his chest. In the silence that fell, her sobbing was as soft as the patter of a gentle rain. Yet the sound of it was almost too painful to bear. Oh, why did this woman disturb him so much? So many thoughts, so many feelings that he didn't understand.

"Listen, I'm sorry," he said finally. "Don't mind me; every time I get shot I turn grouchy as an old bear. I'm just funny that way."

She turned back, a smile playing at her lips. She sniffed and wiped a hand at the dampness on her cheeks. "I feel really dumb."

"No, don't. Come sit back down. Talk to me. I want to hear the rest of it."

Head lowered, Sarah took her place on the chair. She did not meet his eyes. "Where do you want me to start?"

"Well, maybe with how come you're here. I mean, why aren't you in jail?"

"I was for awhile," she said. "That sheriff locked up both Lawson and me, and he kept badgering me all afternoon, trying to make me tell him what the fight was about. But I didn't tell him a thing. I don't think Lawson did either. I could hear the sheriff asking him all the same questions, but I never heard him say much back."

"When did he let you go?"

"Late last night. I kept after him all day, demanding that he let me come see you and find out if you were all right. And he kept saying no way. But then, out of the blue, he and a deputy showed up, marched me over here, and said I could stay."

"Do you know what made him change his mind?"

Sarah shook her head. "I can't figure it out. I wondered if I should trust him, like maybe he was up to something, but I came ahead anyway."

"How about Lawson?" Wager asked. "Did Fuller let him go, too?"

"He was still there when they came for me. After that, I don't know."

Wager frowned. "It doesn't make much sense, does it? Him just letting you go free."

"Well, it's not exactly free. House arrest, he called it. The deputy's sitting right outside. We can't exactly come and go as we please. We're stuck here until the sheriff decides what to do with us."

"It just doesn't figure. It's not like Cal Fuller to go to any kind of extra trouble."

"I think Skelly got to him," Sarah said. "He's behind it all. Do you think the sheriff is the sort of man to take a bribe?"

Wager made a face. "Only if you offered him one. Cal's a decent sort, basically . . . but the basic part doesn't cut all that deep. Who's this Skelly character you keep talking about? And why are you and the old man so scared of him?"

Sarah hesitated. "He's a cattleman from around Bozeman. A big shot; he runs about forty thousand acres and owns a bank, a grain mill, and two or three other businesses there. He's a very powerful man in political circles, and some say he's going to be the next governor of the territory."

She bit off the last few words sharply and then fell silent. Wager looked up, expecting more. "Go ahead. What's his connection to Lawson and Price?"

"Skelly hired them. It's his dirty work those two killers have been doing. They've been following me for the better part of a year now, but I've always managed to stay ahead of them. That's the only reason I'm still alive."

"But why? Why does Skelly want you dead?"

She looked at him for a long moment, then finally shook her head. "No, I can't tell you that."

"Dammit, there you go again. After all I've been through, don't you think I deserve a little trust?"

"It's not that," Sarah said. "I don't want to get you involved. It's for your sake. Everyone who hears the story ends up dead. It has to be my secret, Ethan's and mine."

"I took a bullet for you. That makes me feel pretty involved already."

Sarah shook her head again, vehemently. "No, I'm sorry, but I can't tell you. I can't risk it. I won't."

Wager looked back to his spot on the ceiling. He had been around Sarah long enough to appreciate the depth of her stubbornness. He knew he wouldn't get anywhere nagging at her. Still, it burned him that she wouldn't trust him more. Everything she said was shadowed in mystery, left always half explained. His dislike of mysteries wasn't changing any.

Sourly, he said, "Well, who was Tommy, then? Tell me that much at least."

Sarah lowered her head. Her voice was so soft that he could barely make out the words. "He was my sister's boy," she said. "Little Tommy . . . oh, what a beautiful child he was. So bright, so full of life . . . always laughing and into some mischief. But never any trouble, not even when he was a baby. I remember the day he was born. I ran through the town, stopping everyone I saw and telling them about his being born. I was so excited. They said I made it sound like the Second Coming."

"You must have loved him a great deal," Wager said gently.

"It was like he was my own."

"Where's your sister now?"

"Dead," Sarah said. "Dead all of two years now. There was only Tommy and me left. Just us, together . . . on the run. And then I left him with some good folks where I thought he'd be safe, where they'd never find him. I hated to do that, to let go of him; it was probably the hardest thing I've ever done. But I had to, you know; that wasn't any kind of life for a boy, always on the run, never stopping anywhere longer than a few days, never making any friends, having any fun. I thought I was doing the best thing for him." The words were coming out of her in short little gasps as she fought the tears building behind her eyes. "Oh, what a fool I was. It's all my fault, I never should have made him go."

"You can't know everything," Wager said. He tried to turn her thoughts away from the memory of the boy. "And after you gave Tommy over to these other folks—it was about then that you came to stay with Johnson?"

She sniffed and ran her hand under her nose. "Yes, I sought out Ethan then. I came straight here, and I've been here ever since."

"How long ago was that?"

"Since the fall . . . eight, nine months it's been," she said.

Wager was surprised. "Yeah? You've been around Sheridan all that time—how come I've never seen you in town?"

"I don't come to town. There's nothing for me here." Sarah's head came up, and there was a glimmer of the usual brightness in her eyes. "Everything I need is out there in the mountains. I love the wilderness. Oh, at first it was scary, so open and lonely. But Ethan got me over that. He started to teach me all those many things he knows, how to trap, how to handle animals, how to find your way by the stars and the sun. There's so much to learn, and I love it all.

"I discovered something out there in the mountains. A freedom, a sense of myself that I never knew I had inside me. I can go out running traps for days, weeks at a time, and be totally by myself, no one else for miles around. And I'm not scared then. I can depend on no one else, and have nobody else depending on me, and it's exhilarating, that sort of freedom. It's like no other feeling I've ever known."

"Johnson must be some kind of teacher," Wager said.

She smiled warmly. "Oh, he is. The best. He's gruff and he barks sometimes, but he doesn't mean anything by it. He's like a father to me, the sort of father I wish I'd had. We had the mountains and we had each other, and it was enough for the both of us. It's been so pleasant, so right, that for a while I began to think the past would never touch us again. I pushed Skelly clear out of my mind, and I was almost able to forget . . ."

Wager said, "Until I showed up yesterday."

She sighed sadly. "Yes. God, how much has changed in a day."

Mentioning the time frame made Wager realize something that had been bouncing around in his head, but which he hadn't bothered to think clearly about. He looked at her more closely, and now he could see the puffiness around her eyes, the weary sag of her shoulders. "Did you really sit up here all night watching over me?" he asked, with a tone of wonder.

She looked away quickly, avoiding his eyes. "The doctor said you could get sick from all that liquor he made you drink. I was worried for you. And after all, it's my fault you got hurt in the first place. It was the least I could do."

"Sarah, I don't know what to say."

She jumped up suddenly. "Don't say anything. I'm tired of talk." She moved her chair up closer to the bed, down near the foot. "Fact is, I'm just plain tired. Now that you're okay, I'd like to close my eyes for a while." She sat back down and put her feet up on the bed, close to the edge, as far from Wager's legs as possible. Sighing, she slouched down until her head rested on the hard chair back.

"That's no good," Wager said. "You'll break your neck if you try to sleep that way. Why don't you stretch out on the bed?"

She frowned without bothering to open her eyes. "You're too sick to get out of bed."

"I don't intend to. I'll just move over; there's plenty of room."

"I said no more talk. Especially not that kind. I'm your fellow prisoner, Wager, not your sleeping partner."

"I wasn't suggesting anything. C'mon, I'm a sick man, remember? I won't bother you."

A brief smile fluttered over her face. "I know you won't. You won't bother me at all." She sighed and settled deeper into the chair and was asleep in barely a minute.

Wager frowned at the ceiling for a long time. He was still tired, but sleep felt far away. Over and over, he thought about her last comment, wondering how many ways she'd meant that. Or if she'd meant anything. But like so much else about her, it was a mystery.

Her face, gentled by sleep, was achingly beautiful, as clear and innocent as a child's. There was something comforting about seeing her there, knowing she was nearby, and safe. The steady sound of her breathing was soothing, lulling him, and he felt his own fatigue pressing down on him. After a bit he closed his eyes, and discovered sleep wasn't as far off as he'd thought.

# CHAPTER 14

"WHAT are we doing, just sitting around?" John Nevers said. "This isn't getting us anywhere."

Skelly chuckled around a bite of steak. He gestured with his fork at Nevers's empty plate. "The trouble with you, John, is that you're always in a hurry. Like with that meal there. First-class beef. Might even have been from one of my own cows. And you wolfed yours down like it was some dirty job you couldn't wait to be through with." He stabbed another chunk of steak, and with his knife arranged some mashed potatoes around it, then dipped the forkful into some gravy. He smiled at the concoction like an artist admiring his work. Then he raised his smile to the brooding dark man across the table. "Now, there you sit, bored and impatient, while I am still able to savor the delights of these fine morsels. If you had just taken your time you could still be enjoying yourself as much as I."

"Sure, the fact you took double portions of everything has nothing to do with it."

"John, there's not a drop of romance in your entire body, is there?"

Nevers snorted and sipped at his coffee. As in all his movements, he raised and lowered the cup with a darting economy of action. He never cared to have something in his hands for longer than necessary. He scowled and pushed the cup across the table. "You still haven't answered my question. Why aren't we doing something? The girl and that guy Wager are up in his room with nothing but a fool deputy watching over them. It would be easy as pie to bust in there and finish them off for good."

Skelly beamed. "Pie. Yes, that is a good idea." He signaled

to the waitress. Dabbing at his lips with a napkin, he said, "And then how would you explain your actions to the rest of the town?"

Nevers shrugged. "Who needs to explain?"

"John, I despair for you sometimes; I really do. When will you get it through your head that I am a public figure; I must be accountable for my actions at all times. The cattlemen's association will be voting in a new president soon, and I intend to attain that post. It will be my stepping-stone to the governorship. Nothing must interfere with my winning that election."

"Yeah, so?"

"So do you believe that the men in the association will elect me if they hear that I have participated in the unexplained shooting of two people, especially when one of the two is a young, attractive woman?"

Nevers glared sullenly. "They will if they want that new meeting hall you promised to build for them."

"Not all the men in the association are as pragmatic as you, John. Unfortunately. No, believe me, we must proceed cautiously. Wager and the Martin woman will meet their end, and soon, I promise you. But when they do, it must happen in such a way that my involvement cannot be used against me."

"I take it that means you got a plan?"

"Of course," Skelly said.

"You going to let me in on it? Or do I have to wait and be surprised?"

"Patience, John, patience. Waiting is indeed part of the plan. We must let a certain amount of time pass in order for the plan to have credence."

"How's that?"

Skelly sighed. "I see I shall have to explain the whole thing to you. Very well. It is under way even as we sit here. You see, I have the sheriff laboring in our behalf at this very moment."

"That lard-ass idiot. What's he got to do with it?"

"He is preparing the way for us. Our biggest problem in disposing of our troublesome friends is that they are presently in the heart of town, surrounded by witnesses. So what does that suggest to you, John, that our next step need be?"

Nevers wiped a finger across his thin lips as he considered. "Get them out of town."

"Excellent. But you left out the most important part. We must get them out of town in a fashion that will lead no one to suspect shady dealings. That is where the sheriff comes in. He will take his two prisoners away for us, on the pretense of delivering them up to the federal marshals in Bozeman. He is already establishing this alibi. He is making it known around town that he is perplexed by the question of what to do with these prisoners who were shooting up his town yesterday, and has decided to dump them into the lap of the feds. A believable turn of events, I think. Certainly anyone who knows Sheriff Fuller would readily accept that he would be quick to turn his troubles over to anyone who would take them off his hands."

Nevers nodded. "Yeah, I'd buy that."

Skelly sat back with a sigh, patting his ample stomach. "And the rest, you see, is simplicity itself. Once the sheriff has transported his prisoners a safe distance away, we meet up with him. About the time that his foolish prisoners try to make a break for it."

"Shot while trying to escape, huh? Yeah, I guess folks will buy that."

"Of course they will," Skelly said, frowning as he tried to get the waitress's attention again. The harried woman nodded before scurrying off to the kitchen.

"And then we're clear to go after the old man," Nevers said.

"Exactly. He is the least of our troubles. He is so much of a loner, it will probably be months before he is missed. If then."

"That only leaves the sheriff. What happens to him when all this is finished?"

Skelly smiled. "I leave that to your imagination, John. And to your considerable and unique talents."

A cold smile flickered across Nevers's face. "I like it."

"I knew you would," Skelly said. He stared across the room

and scowled. "Now where did that damned woman go? A man could starve to death in the time it takes to get waited on around here."

"Patience, Mr. Skelly, patience." The light in John Nevers's eyes was like that of a thin candle burning in a cold and empty room.

# CHAPTER 15

AGONIZING pain forced Wager awake. He stretched groggily, trying to collect himself. His head felt clearer, and the throbbing in his ribs had eased back to a dull ache. The ache in his bladder, though, was a pure misery.

All men have their different tolerances. For some, embarrassment is far worse than any pain. Wager was more pragmatic.

He didn't waste a moment on second thoughts. He wasn't sure he had a moment to waste.

Kicking back the blankets, he lowered his feet to the floor. Sitting up took considerable effort. His head spun dizzily, and he was so weak his body seemed to weigh a ton. It took all his concentration to climb up on his feet. Only then did he realize he was naked.

Glancing quickly over his shoulder, he saw Sarah still sleeping. She looked peaceful if somewhat uncomfortable, her body slouched down in the chair, her legs on the bed up higher than the rest of her. A gentle snoring emanated from her parted lips.

Standing up made the wound in his side hurt. Standing still would be disastrous. Spitting a silent curse to himself, Wager crab-walked across the cold floor, located the chamber pot, and skittered into the semiprivacy of the closet. He burrowed far back behind the hanging clothes. Finishing his business there in the darkness, he sheepishly peeked around the door frame. Sarah was still asleep.

He started back. The floorboards squeaked under his weight as he tiptoed back into the room. His head was woozy, and the dressing on his ribs pulled painfully at the stitches. He gazed at the bed affectionately.

He was halfway there when someone knocked on the door. Loudly.

Sarah's eyelids fluttered and opened. She raised her head and looked straight at him. She frowned. "You're not supposed to be out of bed."

Caught, Wager stood frozen by indecision. "Uh, good morning," he said. "There seems to be someone at the door."

She blinked sleepily and rubbed at her eyes. "Oh, is that what woke me? It's not really morning, is it?"

"Uh, no. I guess it's probably afternoon." Wager put his hands on his hips, then crossed them in front of his chest, fidgeting for a natural-feeling position.

Sarah sighed. "I feel as if I haven't slept any at all." The pounding at the door sounded again. Sarah moaned and got to her feet. "I guess I'd better get that." She started for the door.

"Hey!" Wager called irritably. "I'm naked here."

Sarah glanced back over her shoulder, a hint of mischief glowing in her eyes. "Yeah, I noticed that," she said.

"Well, don't open that door yet." He started crab-walking toward the bed. It was a stiff, slow process. He heard her laugh. "What's so funny?" he snapped. "What are you looking at?"

She giggled. "Not much, really."

Wager reached the bed and awkwardly tried to find a way to crawl into it that wouldn't tear his side wide open. He glared at her across the room. "Ha-ha. The least you could do is cover your eyes. Aren't you women of virtue supposed to swoon, or get all flushed or something, at the sight of a naked man?" he grumbled.

She tilted her head back for a second as if considering. "Naw," she said, her eyes twinkling. "Doesn't sound like any fun to me."

The pounding sounded at the door again, even louder. Sarah pulled it open. Michael Court stood there, fist raised, his face twisted in concern. He looked past Sarah, saw the blur of white skin as Wager plopped himself back under the blankets, and his look became angry. "Did I just see that? What are you two up to?" He marched into the room and shook a finger at Wager. "Nobody said you could get up yet."

"What's the problem?" Wager said innocently.

Court dropped a black bag on the foot of the bed. His walrus mustache quivered. "Don't play games with me. You tear that open and this time I'll let you go ahead and bleed."

Sarah came back over. "That's right, Doctor. You set him straight."

"I wasn't doing anything," Wager protested.

"No, only worrying this poor girl to death."

Sarah fanned a hand in front of her face as she settled back into her chair. "He certainly was. Why, I believe I'm feeling flushed." She flashed a quick secret smile at Wager.

He didn't bother to return it.

Court looked back at her. "Yes, you poor girl, you must be exhausted. Why don't you try to get some sleep?"

"That's a good idea, Doctor. I think I will." She put her feet up on the bed and resumed her pose. Her head lolled to one side, and she appeared to fall instantly asleep. Though Wager would have sworn there was a faint grin on her lips.

Court shook his head. "Poor kid. She's all worn out. Sat up here all night long, didn't she?"

"Yeah, I guess she did."

Dr. Court pulled some instruments from his bag, taking care not to make any noise with them. "Pretty little thing. I still say you're a lucky man, Wager, a very lucky man."

"Sure."

"Real talkative today, aren't you?"

"Yeah," Wager said.

Court listened at his chest. "You feeling okay? How's your head?"

"It's still on my neck, but no thanks to you. What was that poison? I may never take a drink again."

"Good, good," Court muttered. He bent and fiddled with the dressing. "Well, then, maybe I've saved you in more ways than one."

Wager frowned. "What, are you a reformist as well as a quack?"

Court smiled. "No, just a quack." He made a quick examination of Wager's eyes, then began putting things back in his bag. "Believe it or not, I think you're going to live. That was a nice piece of work I did on you, Wager, even if I do say so myself. And of course I do."

Wager lay back, crossing his hands behind his head. "So I can be up and about pretty quick, then?"

Court snapped his bag shut. "Certainly. I like my patients to return to normal routine as soon as possible." He smiled. "Makes it easier for you to pay my bill if you're working, you know."

"Sounds good. Would you mind handing me my clothes?"

"Hold on. That doesn't mean you can go galloping off right now. You still need some bed rest. You can sit up for a while tonight, but that's all, just sit. And then maybe tomorrow, if you're real nice to me, I'll let you take a short walk."

Wager frowned. "Yeah, like across the street to the jail."

Court pushed his bag aside and sat down on the edge of the bed. "Just between you and me, Wager . . . what was that fight all about?"

"I don't really know, Doc."

"Oh, c'mon. You shot and killed a man."

"He was going to shoot Sarah. There wasn't any other way to stop him."

Court nodded thoughtfully. He turned to look at the sleeping girl. "The whole town's buzzing about her today. That was something, her facing down the stranger like that in the middle of the street. There are a hundred theories floating around, but of course no one knows the real story." He left the last word hanging and looked at Wager expectantly.

"Just between you and me, huh, Doc?"

Court shrugged. "And the five or ten others I'll pass it on to."

"Sorry."

"And after all I've done for you," Court said, sighing.

"The truth of it is I don't really know what it's all about."

Court stood up, pursing his lips skeptically. "Sure. You kill one man, take a bullet yourself. But you don't know why."

"Sounds pretty dumb when you put it that way."

"Oh, I don't know," Court chuckled. He looked at Sarah. "I guess it's not hard to understand. I'd do dumber things for a woman like that."

"Hold on. I didn't do that for her."

"No?" Court seemed amused. "Well, anything you say." He picked up his bag, cast one more admiring glance at Sarah, and clucked low in his throat. "But I got this to say—if you didn't, then that *is* dumb."

Wager awoke to the soft music of a woman humming. He opened his eyes and saw Sarah at the window, her back to him. The sunlight that spilled over her was delicate, muted, the pastels of dusk. It shimmered around her in an eerie glow, outlining the sharp jut of her nose and chin, the gentle sweep of her outthrust breasts. She ran her fingers through the back of her hair and stretched—a lazy, catlike movement—then turned and flinched as she saw him watching her.

"Oh, you're awake."

Wager pushed himself up, sitting back against the headboard. "I can't believe I've slept this much. What time is it?"

"Almost sundown," she said. "I slept through nearly the whole day myself. Terrible, isn't it? Now I'll probably be up all night."

"Won't bother me. I'm used to it."

"Yes," she said. "I imagine you are."

"What's that supposed to mean?"

"Oh, nothing." She strayed back over and took her chair. "They're bringing us something up to eat. Are you hungry?"

"Was Fuller here?"

"Yes, just a few minutes ago."

Wager frowned. "You should have woke me. I wanted to hear what that fast-talking weasel has in mind for us."

"The sheriff seems a nice man," Sarah protested.

"Sure, he talks nice to women, he gives candy to children, and he doesn't kick dogs. Least on Sundays. But I wouldn't trust him any more than I would a polecat. When you turn your back on him, things can start to stink."

"He can't be all that bad—he said he loaned you ten dollars last week. That seems a friendly thing to do."

Wager laughed. "Is that how he put it?"

"How else?"

"I took that ten dollars off him in a poker game," he said. "And now he's saying he loaned it to me? That sounds like him, all right."

Sarah made a sour face. "That's a lot of money to risk in a silly game."

"Penny stakes, just a friendly game," Wager said. "I don't play for real money anymore."

"What's real money to you?"

"The most I ever made was twenty thousand dollars."

Her eyes widened incredulously. "Whew, you lived high that year."

Wager said quietly, "That was in one *game.*"

"No." She shook her head in disbelief. "You're teasing me."

Wager shrugged. "But, like I said, I don't do that anymore."

"Where is all that money now?"

Wager leaned back, chuckling. "Oh, let's see. There's probably a third of it in San Francisco, a quarter in Virginia City, and nearly all the rest is in one single private club room in Leadville. And maybe five or six dollars of it is in the pockets of honest men."

"Where's Leadville?"

"You don't know Leadville?" Wager's eyes brightened. "The last place God looks, they called it. Down just a ways south of

Denver. It was a silver town. One year there was one hundred people living there; the next year there was fifteen thousand. At one man's count, there were one hundred and twenty saloons and one hundred eighteen gambling houses. Oh, a man could lose himself right up there. One newspaperman wrote that Leadville is forty degrees closer to hell than any other city in the Union."

"And you found that attractive?"

"I don't know that that's exactly the word I'd use. I found it exciting. Interesting. Sometimes amusing. There were fortunes to be made or lost, and the stakes were as high as your nerve could take you."

"So what made you finally leave all that?" Sarah asked. "How did you end up here?"

Wager's face darkened. "That's a long story."

"I don't think we're going anywhere." Then she thought of something and added, "I mean, at least not until tomorrow."

Wager looked at her. "Fuller did say something, didn't he? What did he tell you?"

Sarah sat back and crossed her legs, chewing on a fingernail. "It's not as bad as I feared. They're planning on moving us tomorrow, taking us to Bozeman to the federal marshal's office. At least they're not going to lynch us or anything. Though I am worried about going that far from Ethan. Skelly may try to get to him, once we're out of the way."

"Oh, hell," Wager groaned.

"What's the matter?"

"Get me my clothes."

Sarah shrank back, startled by his sudden intensity. "What are you talking about? You know the doctor said for you to stay in bed."

"A dead man can rest forever," Wager said. "Now, will you get my damned clothes? We've got to get out of here. There's no way I'm going to let Fuller lead me out of town."

"Why does that bother you so much?"

"Because once we're out in the open we're vulnerable," he

said. "No witnesses, no explaining to do. Even if Fuller is on the level, we could still be attacked by Skelly and his men. And I sure don't want to stake my life on Cal Fuller's protection."

Just then there came a loud single rap at the door. It swung open, and Lon Do walked into the room carrying a wide tray containing two blue china dinner plates, a covered dish, and a pitcher of beer with two tumblers. Wager glanced briefly past his friend and took in the sight of Bill Hopkins, Fuller's deputy, kicked back in a chair out in the hallway, a Winchester across his lap. Then he smiled up at Do.

"That smells almost good enough to eat."

"It is good to see you looking so well, my friend," Do said. "When they carried you inside, I thought to myself this time Sam may have gambled too unwisely. I burned incense at the altar, and the smoke would not move toward my joss. I feared for you and prepared the white robes of mourning."

Coming from Do, this was as emotional an outpouring as an outburst of tears. Wager was visibly moved. Sarah looked back and forth between the two, confused, not understanding a word.

"Burn some more incense for me," Wager said. "Perhaps the wind will turn."

Do smiled thinly. "I will do this, Sam. But in the meantime, I think you must do what you can for yourself. The gods are sometimes lazy and may overlook the man who stays in one place too long."

Wager nodded that he understood the warning. He glanced toward the doorway just as Hopkins sauntered in. "What's all this chatter?" the deputy grunted, a scowl smearing his broad, beefy face. "You there, Do, nobody said you could turn this into a gabfest. Just drop the tray and mosey along. The sheriff says they're to have no visitors."

Do nodded, his face giving away nothing. He set down the tray on the nightstand. "I have made for you, Sam, the Chinese vegetables that you like so much. You must eat all of them;

they will give you the strength you need." The two men exchanged a look. Wager nodded, almost imperceptibly.

The small dapper man smiled, bowed to Sarah, and walked out the door.

Sarah came around the bed and looked down at the tray. "I'm starved. What all did he bring us?"

"Yeah, let's look this over," Hopkins said, elbowing up beside her. "I'm near hollowed out myself." He picked up a cut of meat from a plate of steak and eggs and bit off a large bite.

"Hey!" Sarah complained. "Get your own."

The deputy mumbled around his mouthful of steak, "I gotta check this over, make sure the Chinaman didn't try to sneak nothing to you, don't I?" He bent over the tray, picked the lid off the metal-covered dish of Do's chow mein. "What is all this junk?" The steam rose in a cloud about his face.

"Oriental vegetables," Wager said.

"Chink food, huh?" Hopkins grabbed at a hunk of celery, winced, and drew his hand back. "Damned stuff is hot!"

Wager said, "That's the stuff that makes the Celestials grow so straight and tall."

"Huh? I never saw a Chinaman big enough to blow lint from a white man's navel."

Wager just shrugged.

Hopkins sneered and tossed the celery back atop the chow mein. "Well, maybe I'll leave it for you." He grabbed up the steak from the other plate, smiled, and turned away.

Sarah opened her mouth to yell at the arrogant deputy. A severe look from Wager stopped her.

"Nice talking to you, Hoppy," he said, as Hopkins paused at the doorway and stuck both pieces of meat into his mouth to free his hands to grab the door. "I hope you choke."

Hopkins paused and mumbled something back. No doubt it was incredibly snappy and witty, but it was also completely unintelligible, emanating as it did from around two hunks of greasy steak. The door crashed shut behind the deputy. A moment later came the click of the lock.

Sarah turned to Wager as if she were ready to claw at his eyes as she had done once before. "What was that all about? You let him walk away with our supper!"

"Try some chow mein."

"I'm not so sure I'm all that crazy about eating that green stuff either," Sarah said.

"Let me have your plate anyway." Wager leaned over and began to scoop out the steaming vegetables.

"The eggs look all right," Sarah said. "I'll eat them—hey! Don't dump that disgusting stuff on my eggs."

"Don't worry, I guarantee you'll like them. These vegetables are special."

"Why?"

Wager finished cleaning out the pan. "Because of this." At the bottom of the metal serving pan was a .22-caliber double-barrel derringer. The gun was hot; Wager used a napkin to pick it up and held it out for Sarah's inspection.

"That thing doesn't look big enough to stop a mosquito."

"Across a poker table it can drop a man cold. Lots of sharpers carry them. But I'll grant you it's not much use at any range beyond that."

"Swell, then all we have to do is invite Skelly to a poker game." Sarah scowled and picked up her plate, poked at the chow mein piled over her eggs.

"That might not be a bad idea. I need some cards. Look around, I think there's a deck here someplace."

"You're not serious," Sarah said.

"And my clothes. I gotta have my clothes."

"You are serious."

"Of course. What else did you think?"

She shook her head. "You don't want to know."

# CHAPTER 16

"ARE you sure about this?" Sarah asked.

"Mmmm," Wager muttered.

"Thanks, I feel a lot better now."

Wager stood at the window in his pants and boots. His shirt and coat were thrown over a chair. He scratched idly at the dressing on his ribs as he stared outside at the view of the street. His sense of time was disrupted by all the sleep he'd had; it didn't seem possible that it could already be evening of the day after he'd been shot. But the proof was there in the sky. Overhead, the clouds were gold and crimson, piled upon each other and running to the western horizon like waves to a shore. A red sun glowered above a spider's network of long creeping shadows. There was that peculiar stillness that comes at sunset, as if the whole world is caught out for a moment, hesitating between day and night.

The jailhouse was across the street and a few buildings down. Wager had a good view. As he watched, the door swung open and Sheriff Fuller stepped out into the street. Beside him was a small, dark man Wager had never seen before. They started across the street, headed straight for the Shanghai. They both glanced up, right at the window where Wager stood.

Sarah edged up beside him. "What are you staring at?"

"Bad news is what I'd call it. You know that man with the sheriff?"

She shuddered. "I sure do. That's John Nevers, Skelly's right-hand man. A monster."

"He looks like the sort who goes looking for dogs to kick."

"Or for little boys to murder," Sarah said. Her whole body was quivering, tensed like a coiled spring.

Wager turned away from the window. "You got any more doubts that we need to break out of here?"

Sarah shook her head. She said nothing, but the hatred in her eyes was enough answer.

Wager moved back to the bed, sat down gingerly. As he swung his legs up, he groaned and grabbed at his dressed wound.

"Are you sure you're up to this?" Sarah asked.

"A man with no other choices can do almost anything." Wager held a stack of cards. He went through a series of one-handed cuts, limbering up his fingers. "Okay, let's get on with it."

Sarah came over and pulled the blanket up to cover his trousers. "What happens if we do pull this off? Where will you go?"

"I'm headed for Brago," he said. "It's a ways north, up in the gold strike country. There's bound to be some action there I can latch on to."

"Gambling?"

He nodded, his face a hard mask.

"I thought you had given that up."

"Yeah, so did I. But it's all I know."

Sarah stared down at him a moment. Then, hesitantly, she said, "You could come with us."

Wager spread the cards in a wide fan, snapped it closed. He cut the deck, showing the ace of spades. "You and the old man?" he said. "And where are you going?" He did a quick shuffle, then cut again. Cut directly to the ace. "On the run again?"

Sarah lowered her head. "I guess, put that way, it doesn't sound like much of an offer, does it?"

He looked up at her, feeling that tightness in his chest that was becoming so familiar. Her eyes met his. He stared back into those warm depths, sensing all the pain there, the longing. Those dark eyes seemed to expand until they closed around him, forming a shell that made the room, the whole world disappear. A man could lose himself in those eyes, he thought again.

"Well, it's worth considering," he said gruffly, turning away.

"Sam," she said softly. "If it weren't for all this . . . all the troubles . . . " She left the words hanging, unable, or unwilling, to finish.

Wager patted her hand gently. "One trouble at a time, girl. Let's get this done."

She nodded, and suddenly the moment was past. "Are you ready?" she asked.

"Bring him on."

Without another word, Sarah moved to the door. She raised a fist and banged on the wood loudly.

"Whattaya want?" came the gruff muffled voice from outside.

In response, Sarah just knocked again, louder. She stepped back as there came the sound of a key turning in the lock.

The door swung open. Hopkins stood posed in the doorway, his hand on the gun at his hip. "What are you making all the racket for?"

Sarah went back and sat down on her chair. "We'd like the supper dishes cleared away," she said.

Hopkins glowered. "I ain't no maid."

Wager sat up in bed, idly flipping through the cards. He looked over with a grin. "Maybe you ought to try it, Hoppy. You never know, you might enjoy doing some honest work for a change."

It got the response he'd wanted. The deputy stepped closer, his face screwing up in a sneer. "Ha, you're someone to talk, Wager. When was the last time you did any work at all, huh?"

Wager flicked his hands, and the cards opened like a Japanese fan, coming together to form a complete circle. "You make a point, Hoppy."

"You're damned right I do." The deputy watched, fascinated, as the cards moved back together as if on strings. "You didn't learn to do that working at any honest living."

"That?" Wager said. "That's nothing. You could learn that in a minute flat. Here, let me show you something; have you seen this?" Wager held his right hand out with the deck of cards in his palm. He slowly moved his left hand across, briefly shielding the other hand. Then he held out both hands, palms open. The cards had disappeared. He grinned and motioned to his bare torso. "And nothing up my sleeve."

"How'd you do that?" Hopkins moved even closer, peering curiously.

"Oh, I just left them up in the air," Wager said. "Here, you see." His right hand moved as if plucking something out of the air. A single card appeared in his fingers, as if from nowhere. "And here and here." Two more cards mysteriously appeared.

"Well, by God." Hopkins stepped up right next to the bed. "How you do that?"

"You gotta watch real close," Wager said. Again he briefly covered his right hand with his left. The cards again disappeared. "You watching, now?"

The deputy leaned across the bed, his face only inches from Wager's hand. "I'll catch you this time."

"Good."

Wager's hand flicked, a brief tossing motion like flipping a coin. Suddenly in his palm was the derringer. He touched the muzzle to Hopkins's nose. His left hand came up and grabbed the deputy's hair.

"Did you watch real close, Hoppy?"

Hopkins's eyes were as big as silver dollars. He gulped. "Whattaya think you're pulling? This ain't funny, Wager."

"Ah, that's too bad." Wager pulled back viciously on the man's hair. "You know what's not funny to me? Being sold out by the people I know and trusted. You and Fuller are a couple of lowlifes, Hoppy. I should kill you right now and drag your body out in the woods for the wolves to find. Except I know they couldn't stomach you." He looked over at Sarah. "Isn't that right?"

Sarah nodded. Without his asking her to, she came over and slipped Hopkins's gun out of his holster.

Wager jerked the deputy's head back, put his mouth close to his ear. "I asked her, Hoppy, 'cause this girl knows all about wolves. She knows them inside and out, spends a lot of time with them. But even she can't stand your company."

Hopkins's eyes looked as if they would bulge right out of his face.

"Keep your gun on him, Sarah, while I get my clothes on."

She nodded. "I sure hope you know what we're doing." She kept the revolver trained at Hopkins while Wager struggled into his shirt. Her easy, confident way with the gun convinced the deputy not to try anything.

"You're not going to get away with this, you know," Hopkins said. "You got nowhere to run."

"I guess that means you don't want to come with us." Wager took the gun from Sarah. "Too bad, you would have been such charming company. Sit down on the bed."

The deputy grumbled but sat down on the edge of the bed. They hadn't done anything to hurt him yet, and Wager suspected that he was starting to get his nerve back. Wager had hoped to have Hopkins escort them out, but he could see that simply wouldn't go—the deputy would certainly try something stupid. There was only one thing to do.

Wager motioned with the gun. "Now, look over at that wall."

The deputy grinned defiantly. "What for? You ain't scaring me, Wager. I know you ain't gonna shoot me."

Wager shrugged. "When you're right, you're right." He swung the gun in a short arc, connecting with Hopkins's temple. The man's eyes went blank, and he fell back over the bed.

Wager glanced at Sarah. "I think it's time to leave." He went to the door, cracked it open, and peered outside. He felt Sarah brush up behind him. "Are we going to get away with this?" she asked.

Impulsively, Wager turned and kissed her. Her lips at first

were hard, resistant. Then all at once they melted beneath his, grew warm and compliant. She began to kiss back, her mouth moving hungrily. With a reluctant sigh, Wager pulled away. He smiled down at her. "Keeps getting better," he said, and then opened the door and gave her a gentle shove.

The corridor was empty. They moved cautiously down toward the stairs. Wager knew there were only two ways out: a ten-foot jump from a window, or straight through the saloon. He didn't fancy his chances of dropping ten feet.

Together, they went down the stairs to the landing. Wager peered around the corner at all the activity in the saloon below. The place was moderately busy. There were men at all the gaming tables, and the air was hazy with their tobacco smoke. Wager took it all in with a professional eye. The miners were still in town, he saw—big, rough-looking men in dirty flannel shirts and shapeless hats, their hands clutching buckskin purses. They were gathered mostly around the keno, faro, and monte tables, with a few others at the roulette wheel, all fast action games favored by the impatient miners, who had but a few hours of recreation to break up the monotony of their long, hard weeks.

Fuller was standing by the bar, one boot up on the gleaming brass rail. He was drinking beer, smoking a cigar, and looking pretty pleased with himself. Wager had to look around a moment before he spotted the other one, the man Sarah had called John Nevers. He was standing in a crowd around the craps table, sipping whiskey and watching the action, but he didn't look really interested in the game.

Wager had seen enough. He backed away out of sight, pulled Sarah up close, and whispered in her ear. "They're here."

She trembled and slipped her arms around his waist. She gripped him so tightly that the bandages on his wound began to slip painfully. "Now what?" she said.

Gently, he pried her hands free. "You pick the worst times to get friendly." He handed her Hopkins's revolver. "You find a place to hide up here. Out the window, in a closet, anywhere but in my room. Someone's liable to come have a look around. Let him search; then, after you hear him leave, you slip out as quietly as you can. I'll do my best to make sure they don't notice you."

Her eyes looked enormous, worried. "Wait a minute. Just what are you planning?"

Carefully, he slipped the derringer up his sleeve. "Who the hell knows? You go straight out to the cabin and get Johnson. Don't hold back for anything."

"Are you going to meet us there later?"

Wager sighed. "We had to part company sooner or later, girl."

"Why?" she asked. And then before he knew what was happening, she had her arms locked around his neck and her lips were planted on his mouth, warm and hungry, clasping at him with a fury that almost made him forget where he was.

For a full minute they were locked in each other's arms. Then Wager pushed her away. He shook his head as if to clear it. "Sarah, you ask the damnedest questions," he said. And then before she could reply, he stepped around the corner, disappearing down the stairs.

# CHAPTER 17

THE Shanghai was a long, cavernous place, dominated by the ornate mahogany bar along the far wall. Gaming tables took up nearly every other inch of available space. Those who wanted just to sit and talk did so at the three tables lined up in front of the low stage where the musicians played. At those tables now sat a group of men with long, flaxen hair and beards down to their chests. Wager recognized them as shepherds, part of a flow of European immigrants who were making sheep raising a growing concern in the West. The shepherds seemed to keep to themselves, but that was usual. Their occupations forced them to stay out on the ranges for months at a time, all alone but for the company of their dogs and their flocks. The solitude took its toll, and the attitude of the westerners toward shepherds was they ate their mutton with relish, but keeping company with them was another story.

The musicians were taking a break when Wager entered, and the stillness was like the dead calm before a storm breaks. The hum of voices was a low mutter, and the clink of every tossed coin and chip could be heard clearly. All heads were bowed over cards and bets, and no one paid any attention to him as he wove his way between the tables. Only Sheriff Fuller seemed to find anything out of the ordinary. He saw Wager the moment he stepped down from the stairs and watched him come all the way across the room. The sheriff was frozen with a beer half raised toward his open mouth. Only his eyes moved, following Wager as he came over and leaned up against the bar right next to him.

"Evening, Sheriff," Wager said.

Fuller's mouth shut with a snap. "What the hell do you think you're doing?"

"Glad you're here," Wager said. "Saves me a trip. I was just on my way over to see you."

Fuller yanked out his gun. "You just hold it there, Sam Wager. You aren't getting away from me."

Wager glanced casually over the sheriff's shoulder. He saw John Nevers look up suddenly.

"Take it easy. Do I look like I'm running?"

"Don't you try anything. I'm warning you, Wager."

The second mention of Wager's name sent Nevers into motion. He pushed through the crowd, headed for the stairs. Fuller glanced back, saw this, and nodded as if pleased.

"I wish you'd put that gun away, Sheriff. I already got one hole in me. The thought of another one makes me downright nervous."

"Well, don't think I won't do it. Now, where did you think you were sneaking off to?"

"I told you—to the jail. But since we're here, I might as well get myself a drink." He raised a hand to the bartender.

"Watch it, Wager." Fuller waved his gun nervously. "No fast moves."

"What's the matter? There's no law about the way you drink in this town, is there? If there is, I never heard about it." A few scattered laughs broke through the silence. Every eye in the place was on them.

John Nevers came crashing down the stairs then. He paused at the bottom and glanced Fuller's way. If looks could kill, the sheriff would have dropped right then. Nevers snorted and headed out the door. Going to report to Skelly, no doubt, Wager thought.

Fuller grabbed Wager's shoulder and angrily spun him around. "What did he find up there? Where's the girl? What did you do with my deputy?"

Wager moaned genuinely and held his side. "Easy. You're liable to split me wide open again."

"I'll do worse than that," Fuller hissed.

Out of the corner of his eye, Wager saw Sarah slipping quietly down the stairs.

"One question at a time," Wager said. "What do you want to know first?" The bartender set a beer in front of him. Wager picked it up and nearly spilled it all over himself when Fuller clamped a hand down over his forearm.

"Cut the crap, Wager. You start talking to me, and fast."

Wager coolly looked the man in the face. "Take your hand off my arm, Cal," he said softly.

"Or you'll do what?"

"You tough guys give me a real pain." Saying that, Wager simply grabbed Fuller's little finger and bent it back.

Fuller was tough, but not very smart. He tried to act for a second as if the pain didn't bother him. What that was meant to prove, Wager couldn't figure.

But finally the sheriff had taken enough. He slapped at Wager's hand with the barrel of his gun, breaking the painful hold. Then, not content with that, he snapped his wrist up, backhanding Wager across the mouth. Wager's head jerked back, blood flowing from a cut on his lip.

As a diversion it had its drawbacks. But it was working. Sarah was halfway to the door. No one was looking her way.

Wager gingerly dabbed a finger at his split lip. "I won't forget this, Cal," he said. He turned back to the bar and picked up his beer. "I think I need this more than ever now, to wash the blood out of my mouth."

Just a few more seconds to keep them looking his way. He thought about throwing the beer into Fuller's face, but as it turned out, he didn't have to. Fuller slapped angrily at his hand, accidentally knocking the mug from his grip. The resulting spill was something of a diversion in itself. Everyone in the place stared at the foamy liquid dripping from the counter. The spectators wore sad expressions—in a town where the level of thirst never is matched by the level of wages, a spilled beer is aptly mourned.

In the mirror behind the bar, Wager saw Sarah ease through the door and disappear into the darkness outside. He straightened slowly and turned to face Fuller. He smiled at the dark beer stains on the sheriff's shirt and trousers. "I think we could say that drink was on you, Cal," he said.

Fuller's face was the color of an early summer sunburn. His reply was to drive a fist into Wager's stomach. Air whooshed from his lungs, and Wager bent over double, clutching the bar to keep from falling. The pain was almost paralyzing.

"Now, now that I got your attention, Wager, you're gonna answer my questions. Where's the girl?"

Wager saw Do come out of his office and step up behind the bar. He reached under the counter, groping for the sawed-off shotgun he kept there. Wager shook his head.

"Once more, Wager, and this is the last time—where's that girl?"

"I don't know. I woke up and she was gone."

"Gone, gone where?"

"What a terrific question. You really amaze me sometimes, Cal."

Fuller scowled and raised the gun to backhand Wager again. That pleased Wager—a gun used as a bludgeon is a lot easier to deal with than one that's pointed straight at you. He ducked under the swinging blow, pushed at Fuller's arm, and spun him around. Wager's right arm straightened in a sudden flicking motion and he stepped up, placing the derringer flat against the sheriff's temple.

"I believe you'd better think twice before you do or say a thing, Cal. Your brain's not much of a target, but from this range my chances are fair of at least nicking it."

The sheriff's body turned to stone. Wager eased the revolver from his hand and stuck it inside his belt. He kept the derringer digging into the sheriff's skull while his other hand coiled around the beefy neck. "Now we're going to take a little walk, you and I. Nice night for it, don't you think?"

"You'll never get away with this, Wager," Fuller spluttered.

"I wish one of you clowns would come up with something more original to say," Wager sighed. "Let's get moving, Cal."

Fuller's eyes darted everywhere, appealing to the men at the tables. "The good men of this town won't let you get away with this," he said, desperately trying to goad them into action.

"You better hope they're all good—and sensible, Cal. If any man moves they've got one dead sheriff. And off-season elections are such a bother. You tell them, Cal. You tell them to sit still and mind their own business."

Fuller heard the conviction in Wager's voice. He didn't need much convincing. A man at one of the shepherds' tables had stood up and was slowly raising an old navy revolver. "No!" Fuller screamed. "Sit down you crazy bastard! Sit down, everybody. Do what he says, nobody move."

The rest of the men in the crowd didn't need much convincing either. A few chairs scraped noisily, but otherwise the place was quiet as a funeral parlor.

"We'll leave all you fine folks to get back to your fun," Wager said. He started backing toward the door, dragging the sheriff with him. "You want to bet on how long the sheriff has to live, that's fine. But I see anyone move, the game stops right then."

Nobody moved.

He made it to the door, started to back out onto the sidewalk. A few more steps and he could smell freedom.

It was such a near thing.

The doors were just starting to close behind the sheriff when Wager felt a hand drop on his shoulder. He jerked his head around and looked up into the scowling eyes of Dr. Michael Court.

"Wager, what in the hell are you doing? You're not supposed to—"

Court never got a chance to finish. Fuller, seeing Wager distracted, made a desperate play. Suddenly he threw all his considerable weight backwards, slamming Wager into a post supporting the saloon awning. Wager gasped, feeling every bone in his body shake loose and rattle. For a second his hold on Fuller slackened.

For all his size, the sheriff was pretty quick. He pulled free, caught Wager's wrist, and twisted savagely. The derringer dropped to the sidewalk. Fuller pounced on it. He turned, a gloating smile already at his lips.

Court had moved to one side and stood watching all this. He apparently decided he didn't like seeing someone about to finish off a patient he had worked so hard to keep alive. He threw himself on Fuller's back just at the instant the sheriff pulled the trigger.

The bullet zinged past Wager's head, kicking up splinters from the wooden post behind him. He ducked, picked up the doctor's fallen bag, and tossed it at Fuller's face.

The bag missed the sheriff's face, striking him on the chest. It startled him but did little damage. The bag burst open, and bottles and vials and powders spilled out everywhere. Among the fallen items was a gun.

At the time, though, Wager had his eyes on a different piece of hardware. For Fuller was sighting down on him again, and the derringer still had one shot left.

In amazement, Wager saw the doctor throw himself at Fuller again. He grabbed for the gun at the exact moment that Fuller fired. It all happened in a blur. There was an explosion and a splash of red in the air. Then Court was standing there, frowning and peering down at the perfect little hole in his palm. He turned his hand over once; the hole went through both sides.

"You crazy son of a bitch!" Fuller reared up. He slapped the slightly built doctor away like a troublesome fly. Court tumbled aside, smacked his head on the walk, and lay still.

Screaming with frustrated rage, Fuller launched himself from his hands and knees. Wager lifted a knee into his face. Fuller's head snapped back, and his eyes rolled. The momentum of his run carried him out into the street, where he thudded to the ground and did not move.

Wager turned back to see men gathered at the door of the

saloon. He pulled the revolver from his waistband and waved it about menacingly. "Don't anybody try it."

Court was propped up on one elbow, shaking his head groggily. He stared down at the hole in his palm. "Damn you, Wager, you're more trouble than you're worth."

"I owe you one, Doc."

"I'll add it to your bill." Court moaned softly. "Damn, now I may have to work on myself."

"Try some Murphy's, Doc. It does wonders for the pain."

"Will you just get out of here," Court said grouchily. "Nobody likes a wise guy."

"Yeah, I'm beginning to get that feeling."

Wager saw a rider ambling down the street. He turned and ran out in front of the horse. The man was drunk, listing in the saddle. When Wager grabbed the harness, the horse spooked and reared up on its hind legs. The rider rolled off like a ball from a tabletop. He lay in the mud, blinking, without complaint.

Wager was around the horse in a flash. He grabbed the saddle horn and swung himself up.

"Wager, look out!"

Court's warning and the gunshot sounded in the same instant. A bullet whined past Wager's head so close he swore he could feel its heat. He turned in the saddle and saw it all in the blink of an eye. About thirty yards down the street John Nevers was standing on the far side of a leveled revolver. He was crouched with legs widespread, and was steadying the gun with two hands, sighting carefully down the barrel. It all looked very professional. And deadly. Skelly stood a few feet to one side of the gunman, watching with the same distracted smile he might have worn when watching a prizefight.

There was no time for anything fancy. Wager fired from the hip, pulling off two shots so quickly they seemed almost one sound. Both shots kicked up dirt, wide and harmless, but close enough to be effective. He had the brief pleasure of seeing that smile vanish from Skelly's face as he and his gunman threw themselves to the ground.

Wager didn't wait around to see anything more. He dug his heels savagely into the mare's ribs, and she took off down the street in a full gallop. More shots sounded from behind, but he had no idea how close they came.

Pale faces stared up at him as he rode, for the commotion had brought men outside all up and down the street. No one tried to stop him; the crowd merely watched. It was like being an attraction in some crazy parade, he thought.

Or in a funeral.

He tried hard to force down that thought. And was never so glad as when he passed beyond the edge of town, where the darkness of the wilderness arose to swallow him up.

He rode on, clinging to the mare's back, whipping the reins from side to side across her flanks, his mind blank and blind as the enveloping night.

# CHAPTER 18

SKELLY sat in the sheriff's office with his feet up on Fuller's desk. His boots were fine tanned leather, burnished to the color of spun gold. His face was a different color altogether. He was livid.

"You let him get clean away," he barked. "You let *her* get away. Three of you, and you couldn't deal with one man and a young girl. I'm beginning to wonder what I pay you for."

Fuller was tossing shells into a saddlebag. He looked up. "Hold on there, Skelly. You can't talk to me that way. I'm the sheriff of this town, not one of your hired stooges."

Skelly chuckled softly. "Does that mean you don't want the money, after all?"

"No, it's not like that, exactly."

"I didn't think so."

"But it's personal now," Fuller said. "He beat up one of my deputies and played me for a fool in front of my own folks. When I get my hands on him, he's gonna wish he never was born."

"Yes, I see how well you did the last time you had your hands on him."

The sheriff had a dark, swollen bruise on his forehead that nearly closed one eye. At Skelly's reminder, he winced and touched a finger to the injury. "Wager's been around some," he said. "He's slippery, full of tricks. But I'll see to it he doesn't get a chance to pull anything this time."

"You'll take a posse?" Skelly asked.

Fuller nodded. "Lot of bored men around here looking for something to break the monotony. I won't have any trouble rounding up a few. He can't slip away from all of us."

Skelly nodded, somewhat reluctantly. He glanced at Nevers. The lean gunman said, "I'll go along with the sheriff. I want a crack at this Wager myself. He shot at me. I don't let anybody do that."

Skelly said softly, "And then you will see to the rest of it, as we discussed earlier?" He looked pointedly toward the sheriff.

"No problem," Nevers said.

"That leaves the girl."

Ben Lawson was pacing the floor, chewing on an unlit cigar. He limped slightly as he paced, dragging the leg Sarah had put a hole through. "She's mine," he said, "I'll see to her personal."

"You sure you're up to it, Ben?" Skelly said sarcastically.

Lawson stopped. He threw his cigar in the corner and peered over at Skelly. "You trying to say something, fat man?"

Nevers straightened, his eyes narrowing, but Skelly waved him off with a quick gesture. "Just a question, Ben," he said smoothly. "You can appreciate my concern. After all, you have been after her for almost a year now. One has to wonder what the difficulty has been."

"Yeah, well, finding her was one thing. But now she's found. I know just where she'll be. And exactly what I'm gonna do when I catch up to her there."

"I see. And you anticipate no further difficulties?"

"She's all alone now. Just her and the old man. No one to sneak around behind me anymore."

"And you got no one to sneak around behind her," Nevers said gently.

Lawson spun sharply to face the small, dark man. "You just see to it that Wager pays for that, that he pays dearly for killing Tom."

"Oh, he'll pay all right."

"Gentlemen," Skelly said. "I believe we have accomplished all that we can sitting around here. I suggest that you all get at it. It's getting late and I intend to retire. There is a most uncomfortable trip to Bozeman awaiting me tomorrow."

"You taking off, huh?" Lawson asked.

"Responsibilities demand my return. I have been away too long as it is. Besides, I see no further need to hang around this dung-heap town." Skelly's steely gaze took in each man in turn. "Seeing as I have your solemn word that this unfortunate business will soon be taken care of." He turned on his smooth smile. "And I take it that I do have your word on that."

Each man made a noise of confirmation. None of them looked at one another.

Skelly beamed. "Fine. Good hunting, gentlemen." He stood up and moved to the door. There he turned around and glanced back over his shoulder. "Oh, and one other thing . . . should any of you screw this up one more time, I shouldn't bother to make any future plans. Is that absolutely clear?"

No one said a word. Skelly waved and went through the door. It seemed all the answer he expected or wanted.

Sheriff Fuller swallowed loudly and looked at John Nevers. "Nice man, your boss."

Nevers nodded, a thin smile at his lips. "Yeah, I like him. We get along just fine."

# CHAPTER 19

SARAH slogged wearily through the darkness, picking her way carefully along the rocky trail. She had elected to walk much of the way, for the night was cauldron black and she feared the horse making a misstep and injuring itself. The horses would be all-important now. Now that they had to run again.

It took all her nerve to force herself to keep the slow, careful pace. It was very late, and there was no telling how many of Skelly's gunmen were on her trail. That they would come, she had no doubt. Wager had distracted them for a time, but she was the one Skelly really wanted. She and Ethan. They would come. For the past few minutes Sarah had had the feeling that she was being followed. Twice she had stopped and hidden among the rocks, nervously clutching the revolver while she watched the dark trail. But she had seen and heard nothing. Her nerves, it had to be only her nerves.

They were probably closer than she liked to think, though. She knew this because it had taken her so long to slip out of Sheridan. When she had escaped from the saloon, she had walked across the street and cowered behind a stack of lumber in the alley. There she had witnessed Wager's escape. Her heart had stopped completely until she saw him break away and race off on the captured horse. To the south, leading them away to give her time to reach Ethan and take flight with him.

She could still remember the feeling of Wager's arms around her, the way her breath had died in the pressure of his kiss. The rush of sensations in that brief moment had been wild and frightening, but still pleasant in ways she had never suspected. When he held her she had felt her insides melt into a liquid

123

warmth, a flood of longing for something, something unknown. A new hunger had been awakened by his touch.

They were too confusing, these memories, and too sad. For she knew beyond a doubt that she would never see him again. He was a capable man; already he had surprised her with his strength and resourcefulness. But he could not stand up to Skelly alone; no one could do that. Because he was a man, though, he would try. Sooner or later he would have enough of running, and would turn and make his stand. And he would die.

As so many had already died. Sarah shivered in the cold night air. She was always cold, it seemed. Something to do, perhaps, with loneliness, a crushing loneliness that she knew would never fade. Only with Ethan could it be momentarily forgotten. They were the only survivors, and they had only each other. It would have to be enough.

She splashed through the creek, barely feeling the cold water slosh in her boots. She was already too cold for it to matter. Picking her way along the bank, she started up the slope of the mountain. It was only a short way now. The smell of chimney smoke was strong in the breeze. With a pang of regret, she recalled the many times in the past months she had returned here from running the traps and had caught that scent. How sweet the odor had seemed then. Such feelings it had induced in her: warmth, security, the friendship of the old man. *Home*. This nook in the wilderness had proved to be more of a home than any place she had ever known.

But tonight the strong scent of chimney smoke alarmed her. She knew that just as easily as it helped guide her home, it could guide the killers to their door.

It was all different now. Perhaps nothing would ever be the same again.

Her head came up as she heard Barclay bark out a greeting. A minute later, the panting collie was by her side, leaping up on her, running around and through her legs, nearly knocking her down in his excitement. She bent and stroked the dog behind his ears the way he loved.

"It's good to see you, too," she said. "I have news, Barclay. We'll be leaving soon. Going on a long trip. You'll like that, won't you?"

She spoke with a cheerfulness she did not feel.

"Ethan, it's me, Sarah. It's all right. I'm back."

She saw the barrel of the Sharps appear first. Then the old man stepped around the corner of the house. "Sarah, is it really you? Lord help me, you were gone so long . . . I started to believe the worst."

"It is bad, Ethan. Maybe as bad as it could be."

"You look froze to death, girl. Come in and sit by the fire and tell me about it."

Sarah shook her head. "There's no time for that." She told him all of it. She watched the lined, aged face crease with worry and, as she went on, dissolve into total despair.

He was silent through the whole story. When she finished he stood there, his face like a mask carved from stone. His eyes glowed so dimly she could not bear to look into them. "Ethan?" she said, gently.

He took a long, deep breath. "You see to the horses. I'll start to pack."

"You know someplace we can hide?"

"The last place, darling."

Somewhere in the night the wind had taken a turn. It cut back along the ridges and snaked among the pines, shaking the branches with icy fingers. The trees awakened with a protesting mutter.

Sarah shivered as well. "Will we be safe there?" she asked.

Johnson nodded. "You'll be safe."

It was only later, when she was cinching up the horses that she wondered why he had not said *we*.

# CHAPTER 20

WAGER stopped at the base of a plateau and tied the horse off to some scrub, letting the mare rest and forage while he tackled the climb to the summit of the high tablerock. It was rough going, especially in darkness. Loose scrabble kicked free beneath his boots so that he often found himself clinging to the slope by a single handhold, sometimes by a single finger wedged into a narrow crevice. It was exhausting labor, fought inch by inch, and the only consolation was that he could not see well enough to be frightened by the growing distance between himself and the rocks below.

When he finally hauled himself over the edge, his hands were scratched and bleeding and the ache in his side was a knife blade plunging regularly in and out, to the cadence of his racing heart. For several minutes he sat there, chest heaving, until the dust was blown from his lungs and the pain in his ribs had subsided.

At last he raised his head and looked around. There was no moon, but stars blazed all around, burning like the fires of a million frontier camps, pitched on an endless expanse of black prairie. The stars seemed close enough to touch. But of course he could not, nothing in the world could touch them, and this fact pleased him. It was calming to dwell on their beauty, and to know their constancy was something a man could count on; they would shine on, night after night, always breathtaking, unlike everything else that man could touch, could change, could ultimately violate.

Wager looked around until he located the Big Dipper. Then he lowered his gaze to find that one bright star near the horizon, the compass point of the sky. As he stared at the

North Star, he felt a lump form in his throat, a swelling in his chest. In that direction lay Johnson's cabin. And Sarah. He had only to follow the sky, and the star would lead him straight back to her. And then, from there?

How many times before in his life had he chosen a direction, a path with much less certainty of where it might lead him?

But what was there certain about Sarah, when it came right down to that? What he did know about her was only a fraction of what he didn't. The biggest thing he didn't know was if she would live through the night, through tomorrow, if she had a future or if Skelly and the dark shadows of her past would rise up to cover her finally and for evermore.

Still . . . it was strange, but as he gazed at the starlit sky, the troubles of the past few days seemed unimportant. Everything about this worldly life seemed piddling, insignificant, when measured against the awesome grandeur of the stars. Wager felt a curious distance from himself, as if everything, even his own life, was as far away as the distant stars. And if he could but sit here and study on it, he would be able to chart the course of his life with the easy certainty of an observer, standing somewhere far off, watching himself with the same interest with which he now watched the stars.

Then, as he casually lowered his gaze to the horizon, he swore softly. Off in the distance was a cluster of lights, like stars fallen to earth. These stars, though, were moving. Small fires, moving slowly but perceptibly closer. Torches in the hands of riders.

They were coming. Wager was dismayed at the number of fires he saw blinking across the dark distances. He counted nine, which meant that Fuller must have successfully recruited other townsmen to join in the chase. He felt betrayed to realize that those he had lived among would so quickly turn against him.

But then, in an insight born of the objective distance with which he had been examining his own life, he knew it was not so. He had lived among them, but he had made no great effort

to win friends. He had Lon Do, and he had his work, and that
had been enough. He had functioned as he always had, self-
contained, aloof. Safe. If there was any betrayal, it had been
his. The betrayal of possibilities.

Wager shrugged off the realization as soon as it came. It was
something worth dwelling on, but it would have to be at a later
time. Now he had to get moving again. The torches were still
far away, but they were moving steadily nearer. He was glad
now that he had spent so much of the last two days in bed;
there would be no sleep tonight.

He stood up and peered off into the distance, turning
aimlessly. There seemed nothing to aim for. There was only the
cold light of the stars, and the darkness of the earth, a flat,
featureless black like God's shadow, everywhere all at once.
Nothing but darkness from here to the edge of forever.

"Damned wilderness," he said. And started the climb down.

# CHAPTER 21

THE posse sat around a campfire, shivering in blankets while shaky hands raised tin cups of coffee. In the night they had been drunk, rowdy, full of excitement and the thrill of the chase. In the thin light of dawn they were hung over, weary, bored, and mindful of the jobs and comforts they had left behind them. Their heads drooped toward their chests, and the few who talked did so in a scolding murmur directed toward no one in particular.

The only voices truly raised were those of Fuller and John Nevers; they stood at a careful distance from the rest. Nevers kept a wary eye on the group clustered at the fire, but no one seemed curious enough to bother them.

The gunman's dark eyes flashed as he scowled at the sheriff. "You're giving up already?"

"A master scout couldn't track an elephant across these rocks," Fuller grumbled. His shoulders drooped. "Let's face it. He's gone."

"He is if you give up. Hell, what were we doing out here all night? It was just a waste of time if you let him go now."

"What do you want from me, Nevers? I can't force the men to go on. They don't work for me; they come and go as they please."

"Talk them into it. Offer a reward; Skelly will pay it."

Fuller shook his head wearily. "They won't go for it, I'm telling you. They're spent. Most of them haven't ridden this long and hard in their lives. They got saddle sores in places they never knew they had. They're tired and hungry, and most of all they just ain't interested. Wager isn't worth it to them."

"Yeah, but he's worth something to you. Skelly's offered you a lot of money to bring him down."

Fuller covered a yawn with a hand that then moved up to rub at his red-rimmed eyes. "To tell you the truth, Skelly can take his money and stuff it. I've had all I want, too."

"You think you can back out now?" Nevers said. His thin fingers rolled a cigarette deftly as he glared at the sheriff. He flicked his tongue at the paper, then stuck the firm white cylinder between his lips. "It ain't as simple as that."

Fuller frowned. "No? Why not? I'm my own man, I choose where I go and what I do. Ain't this boss of yours nor any other man who can make me do different."

"Wager made a fool out of you last night," Nevers said. "Right in front of all your friends, he put you down and made off without so much as a scratch. You mean you're just going to let him get away with that?"

"I'll live." Fuller puffed his chest out. "When I think about it I realize I would have done exactly the same in his place. Wager's not a bad sort, really. Hell, I'm almost glad we lost him. Be a shame to kill a man like him over nothing more than money."

"You worthless bag of wind," Nevers hissed. "You ain't got the balls you were born with."

Fuller yawned as if too tired to rise to the insult. He spread his arms wide in a gesture of offering. "You want Wager so bad, you find him. Any direction, anyplace you wanna go. Nobody's stopping you. Just leave me out of it."

"What kind of man are you, Fuller? You let a tramp like Wager walk all over you and then you can't be bothered to find him and put things to square." The cigarette danced in Nevers's thin lips. "You disgust me."

"Well, that's your problem, ain't it?" Fuller turned away, looking back toward the fire and his bedroll with an expression of longing. "Just like Wager is. And I'm too tired to give a damn about your problems anymore."

The men were camped on a patch of flat high on the crest of

a ridge. Fuller and Nevers were a few yards off on a ledge trail that cut across the mountain slope, a pathway for mountain sheep and little else. Below them the hill fell away in a steep slide, broken only by the occasional tree or outcropped boulder. Sunlight was crawling down the crags, but had not yet reached the bottom of the valley.

As Fuller turned back toward the campfire, Nevers grabbed his shoulder. "What is it?" Fuller grumbled, pulling away. "We got nothing left to talk about."

"I got one big offer yet," Nevers said. "Skelly made me promise not to put it to you unless I had to."

"Yeah, well what is it?"

Nevers motioned furtively. "Not here. Come around where the others can't see us. This is just for you alone; we can't let them in on it."

Fuller sighed and let himself be led farther along the curling ledge and out of sight of the camp. Curiosity and greed were rekindled in his eyes. "Yeah, let's have it," he said, in an unnecessary whisper. "What's the big money man got to offer?"

Nevers took the unlit cigarette from his mouth, held it between his fingers as he pointed directly at Fuller's face. "You," he said in a dramatic pitchman's tone, "you are simply not going to believe this." He paused then, frowning as the cigarette slipped from his grasp and fell at the sheriff's feet.

A broad grin split Fuller's face. "For a gunslinger you sure got clumsy hands," he said, and bent to pick up the cigarette.

Nevers's smile was even wider as he swung his boot up into Fuller's lowered face. The sheriff's head snapped back, and he toppled over the edge, skipping like a stone off water as he plunged down the slope. A loud, piercing scream shattered the air; then the sound died abruptly as the body disappeared into the darkness below.

Nevers calmly bent down and picked up his cigarette. He put a match to it just as the other men came pounding around the outcrop. "What the hell was that?"

Nevers blew slim trails of smoke out through his nose. "That fool sheriff of yours just fell off the mountain."

"Yeah?"

"Just when we was set to go home, too. Damn Fuller to hell."

"I'm sure that's already been taken care of."

"Well, damn him anyway."

Those sentiments were repeated, in many inventive variations, during the long hours it took to retrieve the body and begin the grim procession back to town.

# CHAPTER 22

SARAH threw herself to one side as the tree branch came slashing through the darkness at her face. "Ethan!" It had to be the twelfth branch she had ducked from that night. The old man was forever forgetting she was behind him, or so it seemed from the careless way he pushed the limbs aside without a thought as to where they would rebound when he let go. Sarah was getting the thrashing of her life.

She slowed down a little, trailing a safer distance behind. It was obvious he wouldn't be careful; he was oblivious to everything but the trail. She didn't mind slowing down anyway; she was exhausted. The old man set an incredible pace. The trail he followed went up and down over the roughest terrain, and she would have sworn they hadn't taken a level step in all the time since fleeing from the cabin. Sarah was more tired than she'd ever been in her whole life, and yet Johnson made no indication of slowing down.

It was their second night walking. They traveled on foot, for the horses packed as many of their possessions as they could lash on their backs. Johnson walked in the lead while Sarah led the two animals. It was tiring and nervous work for her because the horses were skittish and often balked at the high, narrow ledges across which Johnson led them.

The air in these high mountain passes was thin and cold, and the stars seemed so close that Sarah felt sometimes that they were walking directly among them. Under different circumstances, and at a slower pace, she would have found the trek totally delightful. As it was, all she could do was lower her head and keep pushing herself on; it took all her concentration to keep up with the old man.

Finally, when the sun peeked over the eastern horizon, Johnson called a halt. By that time Sarah was all but asleep on her feet. Her head hung so low that she didn't notice Johnson had halted until she nearly ran into him.

"Are we really stopping?" she gasped.

"You don't mind, do you?"

Sarah sank to the ground, not caring where she landed. "Oh, thank God. Does this mean we're there?" Barclay nuzzled up against her, but she was too weary to even pet the collie.

Johnson sat on a stone beside her and filled his pipe. "No, not yet. We did good, though. About twenty miles, I figure, or near enough. That's a good night's walk; I'm proud of you, Sarah."

"Only *twenty*? I would have sworn we've gone halfway to the Pacific Ocean."

Johnson smiled around the bit of his pipe as he touched a match to the bowl. "The mountains fool you because there's so much up and down to them," he said. "Twenty miles in these parts is a far piece for anyone. Those murderin' slickers won't be quick to catch up to us." He took out a canteen and offered it to Sarah. "Here, girl, put some of this inside you."

She took it gratefully, tipped it back in a long drink. Her eyes grew wide and she sputtered, gasping for breath. "Ethan, that's whiskey."

"That it is." He smiled and helped himself to a stiff pull. Licking his lips, he pushed the canteen at her again. "Drink up, Sarah. It goes sour if you leave it in one of these things too long."

Sarah waved it off. "No, thanks. I've had enough."

"Take a bit more, it'll help you sleep. Keeps the aches and sores of the trip quiet when you lay yourself down."

Hesitantly, she took another sip, felt the warmth flow down her throat and expand in her stomach. "You're right, it feels good." She took a larger swallow and cringed, holding the liquid in her mouth for several moments before gulping it down. "Whew, it's nasty-tasting, though."

"I don't drink anything I like too much," Johnson said. "It's the Protestant in me."

"I thought you didn't drink at all."

Johnson chuckled and puffed on his pipe. "Just because you live with me doesn't mean you got to know everything about me, does it?"

"I thought I did."

"Sarah, you're young. You'll grow out of believing such things. The truth is you can't ever know a person as well as you like to believe you can. When you think you know somebody you think they can't surprise you no more. And that ain't fair to that person. What's more, it just ain't so. Everybody got surprises in them."

Sarah could already feel the whiskey working on her. The world was becoming softer around the edges; her eyelids were heavy, and she yawned. "I'm not sure I know what you mean, Ethan."

"You will. You look all done in, Sarah. Get yourself some sleep now. We got plenty more walking tomorrow."

"Oh, no, Ethan. How much more?"

"Another twenty, maybe twenty-five miles." He slapped her knee gently. "But don't you worry, Sarah. The rest of it will be easier, I promise you."

"Where are we going, Ethan? Where is this place you're so sure we'll be safe?"

"It's just a spot I chanced on a long time ago," he said. "You'll see it when we get there."

She stretched out on the ground and flinched at the contact with a tiny scratch on her cheek, a souvenir of Johnson's tree-snapping tours. "Yeah," she muttered wearily, "if I can trust you not to kill me first."

A dark look flashed on his face. "What's that?"

"Oh, nothing," she yawned. Her eyes closed and she was instantly asleep.

Johnson fetched a blanket from one of the packs, brought it over, and tenderly wrapped it around her. He took the canteen with him and settled down on a stump. He took a long drink, then sat smoking his pipe, watching the blue smoke curl and scamper on the morning breeze. The sun slowly eased over the mountains, flashed straight in his face, but he did not move. The flame in his pipe went out, and still he sat there. His eyes focused on something far off in the distance, and it seemed like something almost painful to watch. For, when he finally looked away, he shut his eyes tight and held them closed as if afraid of what he might see should he open them again.

The going was easier the next day, as Johnson had promised. He veered northwest and led them into a string of mountains he said were called the Shandys. Compared to the peaks and ridges they had already crossed, these gentler, spruce-lined hills were child's play. The only difficulty was in wading through dense brush and tree cover, but Johnson seemed to know every deer and goat trail as if he had lived here all his life. They made good progress without pushing themselves nearly as hard as they had the previous day. Sarah was immensely grateful; if there was a muscle in her body that didn't ache, she thought, then it must be someplace she hadn't paid attention to yet.

It was late in the afternoon when they entered the river valley. The sun had barely dipped toward the west, and already the eastern slopes were fettered by shadows. In this mountain country the days always seemed short, as if the sunlight, like everything else, could keep but a brief, tenuous hold on the craggy slopes before tumbling into the dark valleys below. Johnson led them down. The sound of roaring water was all around them, and at last they came upon a racing stream of white water nearly twenty yards wide.

Johnson pointed to the river and smiled. "It isn't far now, Sarah."

They turned north and followed the bank. Here they could easily walk abreast of each other. "What river is this?" Sarah asked.

"Well, it's really not more than a creek most times," Johnson replied. "It feeds off the Missouri, but in the springtime like now, the runoff from snow on the mountains makes it grow three, four times as big. At this time of year the Abby can get high and fast enough to carry off a horse, while other times it won't hardly muddy a man's boots."

"The Abby, you called it?"

"That's just a name I give it. I don't know that it has a real one."

"I think you should call it Johnson Creek," Sarah said. "I doubt there have been many other men to see this place. For all we know, you could be the only one."

"No, there have been others," he said. She was in good spirits and felt like talking, and there was little she enjoyed hearing more than the memories of Johnson's treks into the mountains when this territory truly was an unexplored wilderness. But he would say no more. He seemed occupied with private thoughts, and walked along as if in a trance, his eyes fastening on every feature of the landscape with a penetrating gaze.

Sarah tired of trying to open him up. After a while she fell back into step behind him and contented herself with absorbing the sights of this new place, which to her seemed wild and beautiful. The charging river was so different from the river she'd known during her youth in St. Louis. The Mississippi was a larger and more impressive waterway, perhaps, but it was slow and murky by comparison. She recalled the Mississippi as a river that invited lazy dips, festive picnics, and unhurried boating jaunts, the men in their suits and straw spinners, the women in white summer dresses and gay bonnets.

The Mississippi, for all its size, seemed civilized, a tame river, whereas this seasonally bloated stream was a wild creature, racing relentlessly, with an energy and purpose all its own. It made her blood move faster, just to be near it. And how wonderful it would be, she thought, if she could just take off and follow it, having no concerns but the fulfillment of a curiosity, tracing a wild river to learn where it was going in such a hurry. How she envied Ethan his early explorations when the land was raw and open and he had been free to roam as he pleased, this way or that, and no other man to tell him where the boundaries of his tomorrow might be.

They walked until nearly dusk, following the river up into the high ground again. Overhead, the white peaks seemed to glow with a ghostlike radiance in the thinning light. Sarah and Johnson were still well into the tree line, and darkness settled quickly there among thick stands of white pine and Douglas fir. The river narrowed and curled back on itself in a winding series of switchbacks. Trees pushed right up to the water's edge, and at times they had to splash out into the shallows to pass. The current tugging at Sarah's legs was so strong that she clung to the horse's harness for support.

Up ahead, she saw Johnson round a bend in the river and suddenly stop. "What is it, Ethan?" she asked as she joined him. And then she looked up and saw it looming over her. Her eyes widened and she unconsciously retreated a step. "I don't believe it," she muttered to herself.

Standing before her was a stern-wheeled steamboat, of a sort that she had seen many times during her childhood. It was smaller than the Mississippi boats but still looked enormous straddling the narrow creek, the flat-bottomed hull firmly settled into the dirt on both banks. In shape it reminded her of a barge with a hotel stuck atop it; the main cabin housing was two stories high, and above that was the small square wheelhouse, where the helmsman sighted between the high-rising twin stacks. It must have been an impressive sight once, all whitewashed and gleaming; but now the timbers had turned gray. Trees leaned over the decks from both sides, casting shadows in which moss collected.

Johnson watched Sarah's face, seeming to enjoy the disbelief he saw there. "Well, girl, this is it," he said.

"This is something, all right. But what?"

"This is our new home. The cabins will be comfortable once

we clean them up some. And I doubt there's more than a handful of men in the whole territory who know about this boat. It'll be safe here."

"How in the world did a steamboat wind up here?"

Johnson shrugged. "I imagine they fought it down from the Missouri during the June rise. The high-water time. There was a spell when lots of steamers were exploring the waters off the Missouri and Yellowstone. They carried most of the freight and furs during some of the early time. More than one boat disappeared like this one, I can tell you. Though this is the only one I've come across personally."

He led her up to the boat's starboard side, where a plank was laid from the grassy bank onto the deck. Sarah craned her neck, looking it all over. "I don't know, Ethan. It's so . . . spooky. Like an old castle in a storybook."

"It don't look like much, I'll grant you. But it'll keep out the wind and snow." He walked out onto the deck and back along the side to a cabin door as if he knew exactly where he was going.

Sarah followed hesitantly. "Why have you never told me about this place before, Ethan?"

Johnson tugged on the cabin door. The weathered and splintered wood groaned in protest. "I would have died if I hadn't found this place," he said. "I was trapping these hills and got caught by the first snow without a scrap of food put by. Lost my mule over a cliff with everything I owned on her back. There I was, cold and hungry, without a gun or a knife, or even a prayer. Then I come onto this boat."

The door finally yielded, swinging open with a screech. He stepped aside and motioned gallantly. "Come see your new home, Sarah."

She stepped inside. A stale smell of dust and trapped air reminded her of a cave. Sunlight streaming through the door behind her etched out the details of a large sitting room, complete with upholstered sofa and chairs. On the far wall there was a large cabinet where glassware and china gleamed dully under coatings of dust.

Johnson pulled back the heavy curtains, and suddenly the room was filled with light and color. The furnishings were elegant, finely crafted, and probably very expensive. Sarah peered at them closely. Some of the pieces looked oddly familiar.

"Ethan, you've got a table and chair just like these back in your cabin."

"Took them off this boat," he said. "I've kept them with me all of twenty years now. But I stole them from some of the other rooms, not this one."

She stroked the elegantly carved sofa back with appreciation. "No, it looks as if everything here's been untouched. It all looks as if it belongs together."

"That's right. I left this room alone."

She looked up, sensing something in his voice. "Why? Is there something special about this room?"

"This was the captain's quarters," he said.

She expected there was more explanation than that, but she didn't push it. She looked around, still shaking her head in disbelief. She certainly hadn't expected their wilderness hideout to be so elegant. Already her mind was working, seeing how it could all look when it was cleaned and shined.

Sarah smiled at the old man. "I want to get started making it livable right now."

"There's no hurry, Sarah. We've got nothing but time." He crossed to an inside door. "But I guess the first place to clean is the bedroom, so you can rest up from the trip. It's right in here." He opened the door and peered inside. His face suddenly paled. "Wait there a minute," he mumbled, and stepped through into the dark room.

Curious and concerned, Sarah quietly slipped over to peek through the doorway. She saw Johnson bent over a large brass-rail bed. He had a long white swath of cloth in his hands, and he stared down at it as if mesmerized.

Sarah edged up until she could make out the thing in his hands. An involuntary gasp escaped her. "My word, Ethan. It's beautiful!"

He turned, still clutching the white wedding dress. The long train spilled onto the floor. The fabric was lace, pale white and delicate, as if spun from air and wisps of fallen cloud.

"I told you to wait out there," Johnson said angrily.

Ignoring him, Sarah walked up, reaching out to stroke the long white gown.

Johnson yanked the dress aside. "No, don't touch it."

"I'm sorry," she stammered, shaken and confused. "It's just so lovely."

He blinked and turned away. "Forgive me, Sarah. I shouldn't have snapped at you."

"That dress . . . it means something special to you, doesn't it, Ethan. Who did it belong to?"

His voice was so soft she could barely hear him. "A woman named Abby Thomas."

"Abby?" she said.

Johnson merely nodded. He carefully spread the dress out on the bed again. He handled it as if he expected it to shred in his hands at any moment.

"Where did you know this woman?" Sarah asked. "Why don't you tell me about her?"

He turned back to her, shielding his eyes as if the sunlight coming through the door was too bright to bear. "No," he said. "Not yet. There's a lot I've got to tell you, Sarah. But not now, not yet. Give me time."

"Of course, Ethan," she said gently, and she reached out to touch his arm.

"Could be I've got some more surprises in me," he said softly. "Some of them you might not like hearing."

And before she could reply, he pushed past her and barged out the door. His footsteps plunked hollowly on the deck outside, and then all was silent, but for the low hum of the creek skimming against the foundered keel below her feet.

Water racing past in a hurry to reach some mysterious some-place.

She turned and hurried out into the light.

# CHAPTER 23

WAGER didn't bother to look back anymore. The posse hadn't shown itself once since he'd spotted it that first night; he was sure the men had given up the chase. Not so strange, he thought; he could remember few occasions when the folks of Sheridan could keep themselves stirred up about anything for more than a few hours. About the time it takes a skinful to wear off. Nope, he was about as safe as he could be, considering that was all alone, out in the middle of nowhere, with no place to go, and nothing special in the future to look forward to. Cheery thoughts to warm a traveler's heart.

The sun had already buried itself behind the hills, and he slouched in the saddle, weary and feeling the grit of long hours in his eyes. Perhaps that was why he didn't see them, or maybe he had nodded off for a minute. Whatever the reason, he glanced up and immediately had to amend his thoughts about being alone, because not more than thirty yards ahead was an entire wagon train, and he was riding straight up on them.

Wager blinked, feeling foolish and as conspicuous as a five-ace poker hand. He thought about dropping back into the brush, but saw it was already too late. He had been spotted. There was some commotion around a few of the wagons, and a lone man on horseback was coming out his way.

Wager pulled up and waited. He placed both hands on the saddle horn and tried to look as unthreatening as possible. Some of these greenhorn settlers spooked real easy, and he hadn't come all this way just to be shot down, mistaken for a road agent.

The man approaching didn't look like any greenhorn, though. He was a stout barrel shape, as wide across as he was tall, though there wasn't any fat hanging over his belt. Above the sandy beard, his face was bronzed, and around his eyes was a series of wrinkles like ripples in a pond, a legacy of hours spent squinting into sun and wind. He rode up and stopped a few yards away, raising his hand in a brief wave. "Evening, mister." His voice was flat, without menace, but he looked ready to move fast if he had to.

"Evening," Wager said back. "I hope I didn't upset anybody, riding up on you like this."

"Some folks upset more easy than others."

"Well, I don't mean anyone any harm. I'll ride on through if my being here's any trouble."

The wrinkles came together as the man squinted. "Getting near dark," he said. "You usually ride in the dark?"

"Not if I can help it."

"You alone?"

"Yeah."

"Where you headed?"

Wager hesitated. "West. That's all I know for certain at this point."

"Leavin' somewhere in a hurry, are you?"

"No, just leaving. I haven't decided where I'm headed yet, but anywhere's better than where I've been."

"Yeah, where'd that be?"

"Sheridan," Wager said.

The man nodded thoughtfully. "Don't blame you. Been there once myself." He inclined his head back toward the camp. "There's coffee on, if you'd like some. And supper in a short piece."

Wager smiled. "That sounds good."

The man curled up one side of his lip. "I didn't say it would be good. Between you and me, these farm women can't cook for squat. But it'll fill you. And you're welcome."

The wagons were parked in a straight arrow headed to the west. The man who'd greeted Wager explained that on the prairies wagon trains often circled for the night, but that such practices on the rugged mountain slopes were simply more trouble than they were worth. "No surer way to bust up a wagon," he said, "than to ask one of these farmers to turn it in a tight space. They think everything handles like a plow, go straight while you can, then tip it over and let the horses drag it back around."

The man's name was A. B. Rule, and it turned out he was the guide for the wagon train, hired to lead them across the Rockies. It was the fifth group he'd led to the Oregon Territory, and after this one, he said, he was going to hang it up for a while, stay out west and see what they were all doing with the promised land once they got their hands on it.

The settlers were friendly enough, but wary around the stranger. They'd been out of their element for months now, and uneasiness seemed as much a part of their faces as their eyes or noses. Rule was the only single man in the lot, and after supper most of the men drifted back to their wagons and their wives, barking at their squabbling children, and dragging their feet in a shuffle that had become second nature over the long, long miles. Two or three hung back, and they enlisted Wager and Rule in a small-stakes poker game. It was more an excuse for conversation than it was real gambling, and Wager joined in reluctantly. He played his hands without any reckoning or bothering to keep track of the others' cards. He folded often and won just enough to keep near even, and kept most of his money well hidden.

It was a good-natured group, with more joshing and joking than card playing, and Wager found himself feeling genuinely at peace. After a while—"long enough for them wimmens to get tired of spyin' on us," as Rule put it—the guide brought out a bottle and passed it over their coffee cups. "A little oil for your lamp?" he asked Wager.

"Just enough to get me lit, but not so much as to fray the wick," Wager replied, thinking that he'd heard this and every other drinking euphemism at least a dozen times.

Rule smiled and slopped a full ounce into the oily black coffee. "Okay, jest enough to sweeten it, then."

They played lazily through another hand, which Wager won with nothing more than a pair of tens. The only one to stay in against him was a settler named McAnelly, who'd tried to draw into a straight, something every other man there was aware of as they watched his lips move each time he counted through his cards. McAnelly missed the draw but tried to bluff through it anyway. Wager had to stay in it because he knew the others were just as aware of McAnelly's lame bluff as he was. Wager didn't want to appear good, but neither did he want to look stupid.

Wager showed his pair. McAnelly groaned and tossed his cards down one at a time, face down. He looked around in blank-eyed bewilderment as all the men there counted off as in one voice: "Three . . . four . . . five . . . six . . . jack!"

The settler's face turned red, and he scowled. "Hey, what gives? You all cheating me?"

Rule grinned as he sat back, biting off the end of some plug chewing tobacco. "Hell, Mac, a man would have to be pretty damned fast to beat you at cheating yourself."

McAnelly withstood many jokes and wide-mouthed impressions during the course of the explanation.

Wager took in his winnings, pushed the cards together, and started to shuffle. He forced himself to go through the procedure slowly, but he still felt Rule's eyes on him while he flipped the cards across to the other men. "You handle them cards pretty smooth, boy," Rule said.

"I've played some," Wager said. "From time to time."

"Uh-huh." Rule glanced at his hand without interest and turned his gaze back on Wager. "You know that time I said I was in Sheridan? I'm beginning to recollect that maybe I seen you there."

"Could be. I don't remember seeing you, though." Wager studied his cards. He had dealt himself a full house, kings over sixes. He threw down the kings. "Dealer takes three."

"Yeah," Rule said, as if he'd been talking all the time uninterrupted. "It was in that saloon run by the Celestial. Lon Soo, Lon Fu, something like that."

"Lon Do," Wager said. "The Little Shanghai. Yeah, you could have seen me there. I did some work for Do occasionally, off and on." Wager was relieved to see he'd dealt himself junk; the pair of sixes was all he had. McAnelly was raising; Wager stayed in just to be friendly, wouldn't hurt to let the man win some back.

"The Little Shanghai." Rule spoke the name as if trying the words out for taste. "Yeah, that was it, all right. What kind of work you do exactly?"

Wager shrugged. "A little of this, little of that, whatever needed to be done. You know, just helped out."

Rule smacked his lips around his chaw. "Little of this, little of that, time to time, off and on, huh? That's how it was?"

Wager met the man's eyes. Softly, he said, "Yes, that's how it was."

Rule squinted and peered at Wager the way a poor man studies a salesman's wares. He studied him a long time. Then finally he smacked his lips again and said, "Well, that probably weren't such a bad place to work. I had me a good time there that night, won me some money at cards, even some at roulette, and that shiny little ball don't hardly ever fall right for me." He nodded in a thoughtful way. "Yeah, it was a straight house. I don't think there was a sharper anywhere in the whole crowd." He looked at Wager and added pointedly, "And you don't find that just anywheres."

"Hey, I'm calling," McAnelly cried impatiently at Wager.

Wager tossed his one pair down for all to see. "No sharpers here either," he said quietly.

McAnelly triumphantly flipped over his three queens. "Ha, couldn't do it to me again, could you?"

Wager sighed in mock defeat. "Deal me out this time, okay? I'm going to roll myself a smoke."

"Me, too," Rule said. At a silent agreement, the two men

moved off a little way from the others. Rule held up the bottle. "Like some more?"

"If you don't mind."

Rule smiled as he poured the whiskey into Wager's cup. "I had some pretty decent whiskey in that Shanghai place, too, come to think on it. Joy juice, they called it. Two drinks of that, they said, and you're feeling so good and friendly that you'd start sayin' good things about your wife . . ."

"Three drinks and you'd even save your own mother-in-law from drowning," Wager finished for him.

"Yeah, that's the stuff," Rule said. He squinted at Wager over his tipped-up cup. "Sounds like you've spent a fair amount of time in saloons."

"A piece."

"There was a rumor that one reason the Shanghai was such a straight house was because this Lon fella had a reformed sharper there, keeping an eye out to make sure no other pros stepped in to fleece the unwary sheep. Nobody cheats in the Shanghai, they said, not to pull a card, or slip in heavy dice . . . and, hell, they didn't even let the monte dealers work, except for the entertainment." Rule looked at Wager. "Could it be that reformed sharper was you?"

"It could be," Wager said.

"Well, son, you're a rare breed. I'll bet the number of gamblers who've gone straight isn't high enough to fill one of these wagons. What's it take to do that, to make you change your ways?"

Wager sighed. "It's a long story."

"Yeah, they always are, aren't they? You know, you should have had more of that joy juice yourself, boy. 'Cause there don't look to be much happy in your eyes. There's trouble there. Something eating away at your gut."

"How would you know that, Rule?"

The wagon guide tugged at the collar of his shirt. It was a habit of his Wager had started to notice. Rule wore his shirt buttoned all the way up around his neck, which seemed odd because he was always acting like it chafed him. "Well, let's just say I've known and learned some about trouble in my own time," he said. "You want to talk about it?"

"It's got nothing to do with saloons. Or with gambling."

Rule shrugged. "You can talk it out if you want to. It might help some, you know. Maybe not. It's up to you. Either way, boy, I'm headed across these mountains and I'm not coming back. There won't be any more trouble for you because of me. Anything you tell me goes to Oregon."

So Wager told him. All of it. Hesitantly at first, but as he went along, the telling got easier. Rule listened through it all without saying a word, nodding intently at times to show he was paying attention, but not interrupting. He scowled as Wager talked about Skelly, and he fingered his collar more often. The wrinkles around his eyes drew in tighter, as if he were watching it all play out before him.

Finally Wager drew his story to a close. He looked up at Rule and smiled self-consciously. "And that's about it. A sad story, isn't it?"

Rule made a face as if the tobacco in his cheek had suddenly turned sour. "The way I see it . . . it ain't exactly the story that's sad, it's the excuse for a man who told it."

Wager stiffened. "What's that?"

"Get mad, if you want to, boy. I listened to you all the way; now I'm going to tell you what I think. You can hear me out or not, it's all the same."

"Go on," Wager said quietly.

Rule glanced around in a distracted way, as if looking for somewhere to start. His eyes fell naturally on the men huddled around the cards. He nodded to himself. "The whole problem with you starts with that, don't it? With gambling?"

"What do you mean?" Wager bristled. "What problem?"

"What made you give up gambling?"

"All right," Wager said with an edge of annoyance. "You want to know it all, okay. About six, seven years ago I was working the riverboats, up and down the lower Missouri. A floating poker game that never stopped. I played the suckers for all they were worth, and there was never a shortage of men ready to be taken. I was good at it. Hell, I was one of the best. There wasn't any trick I didn't know: readers, strippers, hold-outs in the sleeve, the vest, under the table, dealing seconds, from the bottom, the middle, anywhere you please. I can make the cards dance in front of your eyes in a shuffle and never move a one. There wasn't anything I couldn't pull, or recognize if someone tried to pull it on me."

"So you cheated," Rule said flatly.

"I didn't see it as cheating, I saw it as business. Only the suckers thought it was a *game*. It was a simple transaction— they give me their money, and I give them a few hours' entertainment, the fantasy of believing they could win some-thing big, get something out of nothing. Anybody with any brains had to see that's how it was, just a fantasy."

"So what happened to make things look different? To you."

Wager took a deep breath. "The wrong sucker came along, I guess. It couldn't have been easier. He was this young boy from back east somewhere. He was just seventeen or eighteen years old, and full of himself, you know, the way men are at that age. He was from an eastern college and had all the mathematics; he knew there wasn't any way he could lose, he had a system."

Rule nodded. "Don't they always?"

"Yeah," Wager said, almost angrily. "Yeah. He was so sure of himself. If he'd just stacked all the money on the table and pushed it across to me, he could hardly have handed it over any faster. He just wouldn't quit."

"You tried to make him quit, though."

Wager turned away slightly. "No. Of course not. I took him for all he had and didn't bat an eye. Ten thousand dollars this boy had, an inheritance, money his father had given him to start a life and business with. Can you imagine that? Ten thousand dollars, what a life he could have made with a start like that."

Rule said nothing. He touched his collar again, then stood still, waiting patiently.

"But he didn't make any life at all," Wager said finally. "He didn't even have any more life. 'Cause he went back to his cabin, wrote out a note to his mother—his momma, for chris sake—and then put a gun in his mouth and shot his brains out. Seventeen years old." Wager turned slowly back toward Rule. "And he's still seventeen years old. I guess that won't never change."

"So you gave up gambling then," Rule said.

"Not right away. I kept at it as if nothing was different. But it was. I couldn't do it anymore, not right. I knew all the tricks . . . but if I started thinking to use one, I'd get the shakes, tremble all over till I could hardly play straight, much less pull off the cheat."

"And you're still shaking," Rule said. "So you been playing it safe ever since. So safe you might as well not even bother."

Wager frowned. "What do you mean?"

Rule spit his chaw out on the ground and made a look of disgust. "Hell, a man who tries to live safe might just as well roll over and give it up. Save the air for someone who's really alive. 'Cause if you give up takin' chances, then you're already dead, and no use to anybody."

"Well, that's a real friendly thing to say. Thanks, Rule, thanks a lot."

"Smart lip don't make a difference neither. You can't hide behind that all the time you're walking around dead." Rule turned in a slow half-circle, sweeping his arm in the direction of the wagons. "No matter how much I bad-mouth them, I got more respect for the lowliest of these dirt kickers than I do for you. Farming ain't excitin'—it's just low and hard, and rough."

"I know a bit about that," Wager said angrily. "My father was a farmer. He slaved all his life over a few acres of rocks and dust."

"For what? For you to run off and play cards on some riverboat."

"I wasn't cut out to be a farmer. It's not enough."

Rule snorted. "You got that right. You're not cut out for it, 'cause you ain't enough of a gambler. Hell, you think sweating over a few thousand dollars in a poker game is a gamble? What about these folks? They've staked everything to pick up and go somewhere they've never seen, on the bare chance that maybe they can make something better there. And they're risking everything that no matter what—come bad weather or sickness or famine—they'll be good enough to beat it, to come out on top. *That's* a real gamble, with your life and the life of your kids as the stakes. And they do it 'cause they know they gotta take risks to go ahead. Or the main reason they do it . . . simply because they can't live knowing they had the chance and didn't take it. 'Cause regret rots a life, it purely rots a life into dust."

Wager's face was dark. The cigarette paper he had never rolled was crumpled and torn in his hand. "I never thought about my father as a gambler," he muttered.

"Well, maybe you should have. There must be a lot of him in you, under the skin," Rule said gently.

"If he was, he gambled badly. He worked himself to death and never gained a thing."

"Some folks just don't get the cards. But at least he wasn't afraid to try his hand. Least he didn't die *safe*."

Wager shook his head. "No, he didn't die that way."

"This girl," Rule said. "If she means something to you, you got to try something. Even if she don't. 'Cause either way, your trying's what matters here. You already took some big steps toward shaking off the safe because of her. But if you run off now, you'll just be running on forever."

"Regrets?"

Rule nodded. "I've said my piece now, like I said I would. It's up to you to decide what you think's right."

Wager smiled thinly. "What makes you so smart, Rule? Where'd you learn about all this?"

"I've had my run-ins with regret," the stocky man said. "Still got the marks to prove it." With that, he opened his collar.

Around his neck was a perfect circle of scar tissue, red and puffy. His thick bull-neck muscles looked bunched in cords, twisted in odd directions.

"Why'd they hang you, Rule?" Wager asked softly.

"For a good reason, if you want the truth of it." He scratched at the scar tissue distractedly. "I watched a man rape a woman. I stood by and watched and didn't raise a hand to stop it. You know why? Because he was my boss. Because I was afraid that if I tried something, then I'd lose my job and my future and everything. So I didn't do anything."

"They hanged you for doing nothing?"

Rule nodded. "Of course they did. They was right, too. 'Cause that was the same as if I'd taken part. Doing nothing's even worse, in a way. They dragged me out and strung me up, and I didn't do nothing then either. I was almost glad they were going to hang me."

"How come you're alive?"

Rule smiled then, ruefully. "I don't know. Maybe it just wasn't meant to be. They weren't much good at it. They left me hanging a long time, but I didn't die, I just hung there and choked and stared back at them. And finally they cut me down."

Wager couldn't take his eyes from the red marks around the man's neck. "And it left you with that."

Rule scratched at the scars. "Nope. The reason I still got these is because the second time made the marks permanent."

Wager's eyes widened. "They hanged you twice!"

"They hanged me the one time for doing nothing. The second time was for killing that man I watched hurt that woman." He stared off at the stars and stuck some more tobacco in his cheek. "They tried me and hanged me for that, but I didn't ever regret it."

"I never heard of anyone living through a hanging twice."

Rule shook his head. "I don't know why things happen the way they do, no more than you or the next man. I jest figure

God didn't want me, and I'm too ornery for the devil to deal with."

"Don't you wonder if there's some reason behind it all?" Wager asked. "Like why did I happen to run into you, right here and now?"

"If you do something, there'll have been one."

They both turned back then, at the calls of the other men. "Hey, come on, we need more money in this pot."

Wager and Rule walked slowly back into the light of the fire. "No," Rule said. "I don't think we need any more poker tonight." He looked at Wager.

"No, I don't."

The settlers made groans of disappointment and started gathering their coins. Rule turned to Wager and stuck out his hand. He smiled warmly. "I don't expect I'll see you come morning."

"No, I don't think you will."

"Good luck to you, Sam Wager."

"Thanks, Rule. But you know, luck's something I really don't believe in."

The guide nodded slowly and turned away, then looked back with a final smile. "Maybe it's not such a bad time to start."

Wager nodded. "Maybe you're right," he said.

# CHAPTER 24

JOHN Nevers had his gun out as he stepped through the door of Johnson's cabin. He moved carefully, making no sound. There was someone inside.

Nevers slipped through the door and pressed his back against the wall, eyes scanning the large main room. It was all very calm and peaceful. The room was dark but for the glow of a single lamp, set on a table next to a large stuffed chair. There was a man in that chair; Nevers could see his legs stretched out on the ottoman, and the smoke curling up from his cigar. Nevers smiled tightly and raised his gun.

"I'd rather you didn't point that thing at me."

Nevers frowned at the sound of the familiar voice.

Ben Lawson leaned out from the chair and smiled at the poised gunman. "I was wondering when you would get here." He pointed to the chair next to him. "Come put your feet up and make yourself to home."

With a scowl of irritation, Nevers pushed his gun back in his holster and walked around to face Lawson. The gunman was stretched out in the chair with the cigar in one hand and a heavy leather-bound book spread open on his lap. "You look damned comfortable," Nevers growled.

"No harm in that, is there? C'mon, sit down."

Nevers dropped into the chair as if it were a tub of scalding hot water. "Where's Johnson and the girl? That's what you were supposed to take care of out here. Or did you forget?"

"They aren't here. From the looks of things, they cleared out a couple of nights ago. I don't think they're coming back."

"So what are you doing sitting around like the lord of the manor? You should be on their trail."

"There's all sorts of ways to trail a person," Lawson said. "I could have sniffed around like a bloodhound, trying to pick up their scent. But in these mountains it could take days, and the trail wouldn't be easy to follow. So I took a different approach."

"I can see that."

"How'd you do? You take care of Wager?"

"Not yet," Nevers said quietly.

Lawson made a sympathetic clucking noise. "My, my, Skelly's not going to be too pleased with you, is he."

"And he'll be just tickled pink when he hears what a fine job you've been doing."

"What happened?" Lawson asked, not bothering to mask his amusement. "Did Wager step on your toes?"

"That fool sheriff and his posse got in the way. They gave it up after one night, and I had to come back with them. It wouldn't have looked right if I seemed too hot after this guy Wager that I wasn't supposed to know that well."

Lawson smiled and puffed on his cigar. "That sheriff does have a way of screwing things up, doesn't he."

"Not anymore. He had an accident."

"Yeah? Poor man." Lawson cocked an eyebrow. "Fatal—I expect?"

"He tripped and fell down. Someplace where there wasn't anything to fall on."

"I'll remember to say a prayer for him."

Nevers snorted. "Don't waste your breath." He scowled impatiently. "Now, are we going to sit here all night, or are you going to tell me what you've been up to?"

Lawson held up the book in his lap. "This. I been reading. Real interesting it is, too. You ought to look it over yourself."

"I don't have time to waste on books."

"I think you'd like this one. It's the old man's diary." Lawson glanced down at the pages appreciatively. "He must have been quite a man once, you know. It's amazing what all he's done and seen."

Nevers snorted again. "Is there a point to all this?"

"What's even more amazing is what a body can learn from it," Lawson said. "Here, let me read you some."

"Do you have to?"

Lawson skipped through the pages until he found one he wanted, then began to read.

*"May 10, 1868. Vinnie and I are headed to rendezvous. A good season, we got us lots of pelts. Vinnie says this is his last trip, though. He won't go back to the hills. He says trapping's too quiet and lonely, and there ain't enough money in it. Money, that's all he thinks about. A hungry kid with big plans. He's always talking I'm gonna do this, I'm gonna do that. Maybe he would, if he ever stops talking. He's more mouth than action. I guess he's right, though, about not being cut out to run trap. He's got big dreams, and I never heard of no one getting rich and famous at trapping skins. I'm gonna miss him, though. He talks too much, but when you're holed up in the snows, it's nice to hear another voice."*

Lawson paused and looked up.

"Yeah, that's real fascinating," Nevers said dryly.

"Wait, it gets better." Lawson flipped through the pages some more.

*"May 20, 1868. Just a few more days to go. We spent the night with some folks called Cornish. Pete Cornish and six kids, all of them sweet faced and friendly, so's they make me yearn for that family I never started. Cornish is running cattle here and has one hell of a spread. They's the first to try beef ranching on this scale around these hills and it looks like they're on to something. A few more weeks and they take their first drive to market, then they're gonna be rich, I think.*

*"Vinnie is so jealous he can't hardly see straight. He goes around the Cornish spread with big eyes and a kind of fever. He keeps saying what all he could do if he had this sort of set-up for hisself. Sorry to say it, but I don't think it'll ever happen. He ain't got the back bone to work as hard as these Cornish folks have. They sure is nice, and they deserve all the good fortune they're gonna have now it's almost time for them to hit paydirt."*

Lawson turned the page and smiled. "Now, here's where it gets real interesting."

*"May 21, 1868. My heart's broke and my head is spinning so bad I can't hardly write this. I musta died in my sleep last night and gone to hell, or else this is all a bad nightmare . . . I purely can't believe what all happened is real.*

*"Vinnie and I said our good-byes this morning. He said he was going on south, I was gonna keep headed for the rendezvous. We went different ways after leaving the Cornish spread.*

*"I chanced on a buck just a couple miles from there, and after I cleaned it out, I thought to take some of that fresh venison back to the Cornishes. Thought that might be a way of saying thanks for all their kindness and putting us up for the night. So's I loaded up the meat and headed back.*

*"My eyes went all confused at the strange sight I seen when I got back onto Cornish land. The family was outside the house, all lined up in a pack, and there across from them was Vinnie, and he was pointing a gun at them. Well, that sight was so altogether strange that I hung back a minute, kinda doubting my eyes. And then, dear God then, as I watched them, Vinnie started shooting. He kilt big Pete first, then his wife, that dear woman who was so sweet to us. I stood there all frozen like, and I didn't think a body could see a more horrible sight. But then Vinnie shot all the kids, too, one by one, all of them bawling and crying and hanging on to their dead folks. Dear God have mercy on me, but I stood there and watched this and didn't do nothing to stop it. It took forever for them kids to die, I think I'll hear them screaming till the end of my days.*

*"If there is a God he has surely damned my soul to eternal fire for my part in that slaughter. For what I didn't do. Cause I had my Sharps with me, and I coulda brought Vinnie down just as easy as I dropped that buck. Only I didn't do it, I didn't do nothing, even after it was over and they was all dead. When it was done Vinnie ran around jumping and singing like he was so happy he was fit to bust. I shoulda kilt him then. It wouldn't have been no different from killing a dog with the rabies, he was that crazy.*

*"But I didn't do that neither. I run off is what I done. God coulda had his vengeance then, if he'd put his strength in my hands, but all there was in me was this cold chill that I still feel now as I think back*

*on it. I run off like a dog with my tail between my legs, and that's just
how low-down I feel.*

*"I don't know if there is a God. I don't see how there could be, how
any God coulda let Vinnie do what he done. But I purely believe in
the devil, cause that's what was in Vinnie's eyes today. He was some
kinda crazy. He didn't even see me there and doesn't know I know
what he done. I pray he never finds out."*

Lawson looked up with a smug expression. "There. What do
you think of that?"

"You read real nice," Nevers said. "But I still don't see how
that story gets us anywhere."

"Nice to know, isn't it. Didn't you wonder what the old man
had over your boss to make Skelly want him dead?"

Nevers frowned. "Vinnie . . . Vincent Skelly."

"The fat man himself. I always did wonder how a toad like
him got to be so rich and powerful."

Nevers said quietly, "I think you wonder too much."

"Take it easy, Nevers. You and I aren't going to tangle."

"No? Why not?"

"Because," Lawson said with a confident smile. "No point.
Nobody would win."

"That's how you see it."

"That's how it is."

They stared at each other, matching smile for smile. There
was no warmth on either face. Finally, Nevers shrugged and
looked off in a bored fashion. "I still don't see how this book
reading helps us find the old man and the girl," he said.

Lawson patted the diary affectionately. "Because there's
more in here, another part about a place where Johnson and
Skelly holed up that winter. In an old steamboat that got stuck
up in the hills when the high water fell. That's where they'll
be."

"If you're so sure of that, then why aren't you looking for
that steamboat?"

"I thought of a way to make it easier," Lawson said. "You

could send a telegraph to your boss, fetching him back up here. He knows where that boat is, he was there with Johnson. He could lead us straight there. Anyway, I sort of thought he might enjoy being there when we finally catch up to them. He's been worried over the girl and Johnson a long time; he might appreciate the personal touch when we finally make an end to it all."

"He might," Nevers said. "He might at that." He sat back and scratched at his chin as he considered the idea. "But before I send any wire to take the boss away from his business, I gotta be damned sure we're going to find those two where you say they'll be. What makes you so certain they're hiding in this old wrecked boat?"

Lawson held up a single piece of paper. "Because the girl left this."

Nevers leaned forward, frowning. His lips moved slowly as he read with some obvious difficulty the brief message scrawled in a bold but definitely feminine hand:

*Sam—*

*I pray that you are alive and unhurt and will find this. Ethan and I are fleeing into the hills. He won't tell me where we are going, except that it is north and the last place Skelly would expect to find him. Please make no effort to follow us. There is no way to tell you how I feel about you, and the gratitude for all you've done. You are a special man, and I will always have a warm place in my heart when I think of you. If only things were different . . .*

*Sarah*

Nevers finished and sat back with a weary sigh. "Yeah, so?"

Lawson grinned. "You don't read very well, do you?"

"What of it?" Nevers said sharply.

Lawson held up the diary. "The answer is all in here. If you would read this—if you *could* read this—you would know that this boat is where they've gone."

"C'mon, spit it out. Why there?"

"It's just like she said," Lawson replied. "Because, believe me, this boat is the last place on earth Skelly would expect Johnson to ever go."

# CHAPTER 25

SARAH lay in the darkness, listening to the river hum as it raced below the keel of the stranded boat. She was weary from all the cleaning and rearranging they had done to make the cabin livable, but her mind would not let sleep come. Thoughts, memories, dreams, they all drifted together, becoming tangled, interwoven. There was no reality in the darkness but that of her imagination, a reality fashioned of renewed possibilities, of second chances, or of first chances taken, the sweetly impossible what might have been.

*If only things were different . . .*

She remembered her sister Ellen. So easy life had seemed for her. While Sarah had run wild exploring caves and rivers, seeking mischief and games, in all ways trying to be the son her father had so desired but never had, Ellen blossomed early into what she would always be: a fine, delicate lady. She had never tried to be anything other than what she was, and her father had not loved her any less for it. In some ways, Sarah believed, their father had loved her more because of it.

Death had been easy for Ellen, too. For when Tom Price put a bullet through her heart, it was at least mercifully quick, and painless. The pain was left for those who would mourn her.

And that was Sarah. For Ellen's husband Mark had been killed almost in the same instant. Fate had offered him the same dubious gift of a mercifully quick death. He didn't even have time to realize that it was his mistake that had brought death upon them.

Mark Johnson, how like his father he had been, Sarah thought. Though Ethan's strength was in his hands and body, while Mark's strength had been in his quick and insightful

162

mind, in his hunger for the truth, and the dogged determination with which he pursued it. Sarah could recall so clearly that day at the family gathering when Ethan, for the first time, told the story of how Vincent Skelly had made his fortune through an act of murder. She remembered how the excitement had seized Mark, how he left them all to race back to his newspaper office, and began to pursue the story that would change all their lives.

And end some of them. It was a week later when Mark made his terrible mistake. He had gathered his story; it was ready to be printed. But because of his principles, he had one final task to perform; he marched into Skelly's office and presented him with the story, gave him the chance to confirm or deny. Skelly made no reply at all. Not then. It was later that very afternoon when two gunmen named Ben Lawson and Tom Price arrived with Skelly's answer.

By chance, Ellen and Mark's son had been with Sarah, and so was spared. When she learned what had happened, Sarah took Tommy and fled. She was fully aware that a man who would kill one entire family to gain his desires would not hesitate to kill in such numbers again. So she and Tommy ran. It was their only choice.

Little Tommy. The pain in her heart was almost unbearable when she thought of him. What a fine, brave little man he had been. The day she told him his parents were dead, he had thought for a minute, then asked simply: "Are Mommy and Daddy together in heaven?"

"Yes, dear. They're together. Always and forever."

The boy nodded solemnly. "Good, then they'll be happy."

He had refused to cry until later, when he thought he was alone and Sarah would not hear him. But she had, and she would remember that sound for the rest of her life. Always and forever.

Dead. All of them dead. Tommy had finally rejoined his parents. Sarah hoped, she prayed, that there was a heaven, that they truly were together and would be happy. There had to be a place for happiness somewhere. It seemed there was none anywhere on this earth.

Here and there in her thoughts appeared another face, that of Sam Wager. He was a man she barely knew, yet in some odd way she felt she had known him all her life. She wondered if now he was dead, too. It seemed most likely. Even if he was alive, she could not think of him that way. It was easier, less painful, to believe him dead. For one way or another, she knew she would never see him again.

So much death. So many lives abruptly ended when they had barely begun. The waste of it, the appalling unfairness, was too much to bear. There was a sour emptiness inside her where she knew life would never grow again. And the tears that welled in her eyes were all the more bitter and painful in that she did not release them. She had cried all she could. Tears did not help, no more than dreams did. Dreams were a small death in themselves, for they made you believe in what could not be. The truth was all she had now, and it had to be faced each and every day, no matter how unpleasant. It would have to be enough.

Thinking this, Sarah's mind went to the old man. There was something about the truth, something in the past, which he could not face. Coming to this place had been for him a form of surrender, it seemed. In the past few days he had done little work, had simply sat and stared with blank eyes at something Sarah could not see.

The bed squeaked as Sarah got up and walked to the door. He was still there as she had left him earlier. There were no candles or lamps in the room, only the banked fire on the hearth. The glow flittered through the open spaces, barely scratching at the darkness. Johnson sat in a large, stiff-backed chair, his legs stretched out before him. His head was slumped over, but his eyes were open, staring into the fire. He looked as if he had not moved at all in the time Sarah had been tossing and turning with her own thoughts.

She went up behind him and gently touched his shoulder. "Ethan?"

He didn't look up. "I guess you expect to hear it all, don't you?" he said.

"I want to understand."

His gray shaggy head nodded, almost imperceptibly. His eyes still watched the flames, not moving, not even as she stepped away to take the chair across from him. He stared into the fire as if the past were contained there, flickering briefly the way the flames danced and sputtered. His voice was only a whisper, but it was as if they were the only two people in the world, and she heard him clearly.

"It was so long ago," he said. "You'd think something that far gone shouldn't matter anymore. I don't know why it still does. I thought maybe this time it would be different. But it's not. It's worse, if anything. I guess 'cause now, now that I'm near the end of my life, I know I ain't ever made up for it, ain't ever found a way to stop hurting because of it, and now I know I never will. I can look back over my life, and I can see everything going off in one direction all 'cause of what happened here. Maybe it could have all been different, all been better, if only . . ."

He paused and took a deep breath, as if gathering himself to tell the story. Sarah watched silently. She did not understand any of it yet, but she did not interrupt, she let him tell it in his own way.

"I told you what it was like the first time I come here," Johnson said finally. "It was a winter straight out of your nightmares. The wind blew straight from hell, and it snowed every day for weeks at a time. The drifts went halfway up the trees; the horses just dropped into them like they had fallen into some lake. They might have lasted awhile if we could have camped somewhere out of the wind, not had to force our way through that snow . . . but we couldn't do that; there weren't no food. The horses couldn't take it, their hearts just burst from trying to wade through that snow. Like kicking in quicksand.

"I had my snowshoes, so I could make my way all right, but I didn't have no food either. My stomach was clear back against my backbone, and it gnawed at me something awful. I thought at first I could sit out the blizzard, so I dug in and waited. But that storm went on forever, and finally I knew I had to try to make my way out through it to the lower ground or some sheltered pass somewhere or I would starve to death where I sat.

"I don't know how many days I walked. I don't remember much about that at all; it was just one step after another, and nothing but the snow in my face. I knew I was done for, I had already decided I was gonna die and so what, at least I wouldn't be cold no more. And just when I was ready to lie down and close my eyes for good, I walked straight into this boat here, walked blind right up to it and fetched a blow to my head against the hull. I felt around until I figured out what it was, though I couldn't really believe. I found my way up onto the deck and started pounding on a door, and then I guess I just passed out 'cause I don't remember being dragged inside."

"There were people here on the boat?" Sarah said incredulously.

"There was just two," Johnson said. "One was the captain, Captain Benjamin Salem."

"And the woman?"

Johnson nodded. "Abby. The captain's woman."

"My God, what were they doing here?"

"I don't know how long they'd been here, but it must have been least a year. Maybe even longer. When the boat ran aground I guess it must have been a terrible crash. The captain broke both his legs, and neither one of them set. They just hung down like puppet legs with the strings broke; it was bad, he couldn't take a step. The crew, what there was left after the crash, took off into the hills, trying to find their way back."

Sarah scowled. "They ran off and left him helpless like that. What sort of men were they?"

"No different from men anywhere, I expect. They had their own lives to think of, and nobody who saw Salem with those broke legs thought he would live long anyways."

"I hope they all got lost and never found their way back," Sarah said.

"Likely they did. I never heard tell of any, and you'd think a story like they had to tell would get around. But maybe considering what they done, they just thought better never to talk about it."

"I should think so."

For the first time, Johnson moved his gaze to look at her. There was so much pain in his eyes that she could not meet them. He slowly turned back, found his point in the fire, and picked up his story again.

"I was so far gone I damned near died anyway. I don't know how Abby nursed me through it. And her with one sick man to tend for, already. She had to see to Salem every day. He was still up in the wheelhouse; there wasn't any way to move him. His legs never healed up right; they swole up and turned colors. They smelled like they died and were rotting right off him. He just sat there in the same place, day after day, couldn't hardly move a muscle. That wheelhouse was horrible, full of the stink of his filth and the smell of those legs. Abby did what she could to clean up after him, but it was still someplace you'd make a deal with Satan to avoid.

"I don't know how it was he lived so long. By all rights he shoulda been dead a long time before that. Unless it was the drink. He didn't do anything but sit there and stare down the river and drink. There was a hold full of whiskey in crates. Abby took a bottle to him every day, and left some food, though he wouldn't eat any more than it took to keep him alive.

"And he wouldn't say a word to her. He hadn't talked in the whole time they'd been here. She thought he'd forgot how to.

He was just like some wild animal in a cage, trapped and waiting to die.''

Sarah gasped. "How horrible. And how lonely for her, for Abby.''

Johnson closed his eyes, as if his point in the fire had suddenly grown too bright to stare at. When he began again, the words came out in fits and starts, as if he were having trouble breathing. "There was a powerful lonesomeness in that woman,'' he said. "The loneliness ate away at her insides the same way the rot ate away at Salem's legs. Women can't take being alone as easy as a man.'' He glanced at Sarah briefly. "At least most women can't. Abby sure weren't made for it. After I was healed up and able to talk and move about, she latched on to me and wouldn't let go. We were together every minute of the day; she wouldn't let me outta her sight.

"I was still a young man then. I hadn't met Mark's mother yet. I hadn't had anything to do with women up till then. So with all her attentions and . . . hungers and everything, well, she shook me up pretty good. All that time, and it seemed like there wasn't anybody else in the whole world but us, and so . . .''

"You became lovers?'' Sarah said.

Johnson's bearded chin dipped toward his chest. "She seemed so lovely and fine, delicate as a flower.''

"It's not something to be ashamed of, Ethan,'' Sarah said gently.

Johnson said, "She was also crazy as a loon.''

Sarah flinched, blinking as if she had just sensed the same harsh light the old man saw in the flames. "I didn't realize at first how crazy she was,'' Johnson continued. "Maybe I was a bit touched myself. It all seemed so unreal, somehow, that time. She talked and talked, and I didn't know what she meant all times, so I didn't catch on right away. It wasn't until she started to talk about it all the time that I realized what she wanted from me. That what she was talking about was murder.''

"Oh, no, Ethan.''

He didn't look at her. Johnson went on, the words coming out faster now. "I told you she was crazy. She was afraid of Salem. She got it in her head that he had cast some kind of spell over her, that she could never be free until he was dead. He was like some kind of ghost, sitting up there in the wheel-house, haunting us before he was even dead. It was spooky, because there didn't seem no life in him, there didn't seem any reason why he hadn't died a long time before. I said it was like we were the only ones in the world, but of course, we weren't really alone. He was always there, always sitting over our heads. The thought of that, and all her crazy talk, after a while it started to get to me. I started to be afraid of him, too. I knew we couldn't ever be together, not in the whole way we wanted, until he was dead."

Sarah started to shake her head. She put her hands to her ears as if to hold her head still, but it would not stop.

"So, finally," Johnson said, "after all that time of her begging me to do it, I took my gun and I went up there to the wheelhouse. I was shaking so bad I almost fell off the ladder and killed myself on the way. I slipped in real quiet and went up behind him. But for the first time, he turned and looked at me. And there wasn't any craziness in his eyes. He said real plain, 'Why'd it take you so long?' "

Johnson fell silent for a moment. He didn't move; it seemed he didn't even breathe. His eyes were closed so tightly it seemed they had receded into his head. Then at last, a soft sigh escaped him. He turned to Sarah, even though she was not looking at him.

"And I did it," he whispered. "I touched my gun to his head and blew him straight to God."

Sarah moaned, burying her face in her hands. It seemed she did have tears yet to spill, after all.

The old man went on in that strange, hushed tone, "And when I saw him dead like that, I knew . . . I knew she'd been right. 'Cause he didn't look no different. Except for the hole in his head. He was still sitting there, looking out over the river, just like he'd always done. And the look in his eyes was just the same."

Johnson turned away. Sarah's sobbing was a low beat against the droning melody of the humming river. The fire had burned low, and the darkness was close around them.

"Then I come back down," Johnson said. "I found Abby in that bedroom. She looked at me with the gun in my hand and blood on my clothes, and she knew right off that I had done it.

"She had that white dress spread out on the bed, and she was stroking it, smoothing it all out, and kind of humming to herself, happy like. 'I done it,' I told her. 'I kilt the captain.' She looked at me all funny, and she said, 'The captain can't be dead. I'm the captain's woman.' She played with that dress some more and said, 'We're going to be married as soon as we reach port.'"

Sarah looked up, a shiver racing down her spine. "Oh, no."

The old man continued as if he hadn't heard, as if he were talking to himself. "I argued with her some, and took her in my arms and tried to shake the sense into her. She said, 'Don't touch me. I told you, I'm the captain's woman.' I told her again that the captain was dead. And it got through to her, and she started to scream. She screamed and screamed, and then before I could do anything, she ran out the door and right off the boat, started to run through the snow down the river ice. I went out, but she was already twenty or thirty yards off, and before I made up my mind what to do they caught her."

"Who, Ethan?" Sarah asked softly. "Who caught her?"

"The wolves," he said. "It was the strangest thing, it was like they had been there all along, just waiting. Usually wolves won't do that, they won't attack a living person. People talk about such things, but they're just stories to scare the children. But this time they did. Maybe it was that they were crazy-starved on account of the bad winter. Or maybe they smelled all that death on her. Anyway, she hadn't gotten but a little ways, and the first one dragged her down. She had stopped screaming then, and she didn't make a sound. Then they was all on her, a whole pack, ten or twenty of them. They tore her clear apart."

"Ethan." Sarah ached for him. She longed to touch him, to offer him some words of comfort, but she could neither move nor speak.

He looked at her, and at last it was as if the mood had broken. His voice became stronger. "I took off that very day," he said. "I couldn't spend another night here. And I walked all the way in from the hills without seeing a single wolf. I never came back but the one time, and Skelly was with me then. That was when we got the chairs and stuff. But I couldn't stay, not even then. Skelly, he went up to the wheelhouse, and he said . . . he said there's nothing up there of the captain, no bones, nothing. There's no more of him than there is of Abby. I don't know if he was trying to spook me or not. I can't go up there, not even now."

Sarah nodded, but said nothing. There was nothing to say. She sat back and closed her eyes, pulling a blanket around her and curling up like a child.

Johnson turned back to the fire, and his head dropped to his chest. For a long time he sat unmoving. The fire burned down, and the darkness crept closer around them. When the shadows finally reached him, he looked up and his lips quivered as if in a smile of welcome.

# CHAPTER 26

AROUND noon it began to rain, a slanting downpour that lashed at Wager's face and left him soaked. Lightning arced across the skies, briefly showing the mountain peaks, brooding under dark cowls of scudding cloud. Wager shivered and pulled his coat tighter around him. He felt at home in the storm; the world around him was no darker than his thoughts.

Sheridan was closed up against the weather, as quiet as though deserted. Wager skirted around the edge of town without much worry of being seen and recognized. He headed north down the trail to Johnson's cabin, the familiar path where it had all begun. Where or how it would end, he tried not to think about. He tried his best not to think at all. It was something he felt he was getting pretty good at.

Two hours later, he tied off his horse among the familiar pines and approached the cabin on foot. It all looked quiet. The house was dark, empty looking. Outside the yard, the buckboard still stood exactly as he had left it so long before. The crate was still in the back. Poor kid, Wager thought, everyone too busy even to bury you. He hoped the boy had gotten better attention when he had lived.

He sat and watched for a good while, but there was no sign of activity anywhere. Finally, he knew he would have to try it. Ducking into a low crouch, he ran across the clearing. His heart pumped faster than his legs, and it seemed like half a lifetime before he finally threw himself down along the east wall of the cabin. The storm had passed, and the rain had gentled to a steady trickle. The cold mist tickled his upturned face as he eased up to peer through a window.

At first it looked innocent enough, but then as his eyes

adjusted to the dim light, he saw what looked like the signs of a struggle. A table and chairs lay overturned, and a section of the big throw rug was bunched up and folded back on itself. Frowning, Wager looked closer, and saw a large dark object sprawled out over the floor. His heart finally slowed a bit—in fact, it seemed to momentarily stop.

It was a man's body.

Warily, Wager edged around to the front of the house, sidled up and glanced through the open door. He could see the man clearly now. It was Lawson. He lay stretched out on his face, legs and arms askew. A revolver was a few inches from his right hand, as if he had been holding it when someone put him down.

Wager pulled his own gun before he slipped through the door. On tiptoe, he crossed the large main room and bent down to examine the body. His brow wrinkled as he encountered an unexpected warmth. He drew back in surprise, but before he could move a husky voice barked out behind him.

"Hold it right there, Wager! You make one move, it'll be your last."

Wager did his impression of a rock. From the corners of his eyes, he saw the two men step out from the shadows in the far corners of the room. One man was tall and plump, the other small, dark, whipcord lean. "Okay, you can drop that gun now," the second one said.

Wager quickly figured the odds. It didn't take long. He tossed his gun onto the floor.

"Fine. Now raise those hands."

Sighing, Wager slowly straightened and raised his hands above his head. The plump man came around in front, inspecting him with frank interest. "Well, well," he said. "It's about time we finally met, don't you think, Wager? My name's Vincent Skelly. This is my friend and associate, John Nevers." Skelly glanced down and smiled. "Him—I think—you already know."

The body at Wager's feet came suddenly to life. Lawson

rolled over and grinned that thin-edged smile. "What's the matter, Wager? Where's that sharp tongue of yours?"

"Surprise parties leave me cold. You really shouldn't have."

Skelly laughed. "You're a surprise to me, Wager. I didn't think we'd ever see you again. You could have been a long ways from here by now."

"Now there's a thought," Wager mumbled.

Lawson climbed to his feet, dusted himself off. His eyes had the warmth of a lizard's. "I'm not at all sorry you decided to come back. You and I have some unfinished business."

"That's right. You still owe me fifty dollars."

The lizard eyes gleamed. "Where you planning on spending it, Wager?"

Wager sighed. "Good point," he said.

# CHAPTER 27

THEY moved him outside. The dark clouds were splitting off, and a hint of blue sky peeked through the widening seams. During the storm the world had appeared a bleak wash of grays and blacks, but now color was reemerging. Raindrops glistening on the wildflowers made the buds sparkle as bright as any jewel. Wager was glad. At least he would have something pretty to look at before his eyes closed forever.

From the way Lawson kept grinning at him, he figured that wouldn't be long.

Nevers moved off into the trees at the far side of the clearing, then reappeared leading three horses. "We were just about to take a small journey when we heard you coming," Skelly said. "How fortunate that you turned up when you did."

"Yeah, it would have been terrible if I'd missed you."

"Why did you come back, Wager? You were clean away. Oh, we would have found you eventually. But considering Ben's dubious record of following the girl, it could have taken a long, long time to catch up to you."

"Maybe I just didn't want to spend that time looking back over my shoulder," Wager said.

"There has to be more to it than that."

"It's the girl," Lawson said. "I think he went sweet on her." He rubbed a hand down his bearded face, as if the smile there was bothering him. "Not that I blame you that much, Wager. She is a sight. I wouldn't mind getting some of that myself."

A hard look settled over Wager's face at the thought of Lawson with his hands on Sarah. He met the gunman's eyes. "I'll see you in hell first."

"You'll be there waiting long before me," Lawson replied.

"Fact is, I don't see any reason why you shouldn't head that way right now."

Skelly looked back and forth between the two of them and made a low clucking noise in his throat. "Now, this is an interesting development I wasn't aware of," he said. "Hmmm, so you and little Sarah have something between you, huh?"

"Had," Lawson said, as he raised his gun, leveling it at Wager's face. "The poor girl's gonna have to sleep alone from now on. But don't you worry, Wager. I'll see to it that pretty young thing don't get cold."

"Lawson, put that gun down," Skelly ordered. "No killing him until I say so."

"What the hell, he's no use to us."

"So you say. But I'm the one giving the orders here," Skelly barked. "Now stop it."

Disappointment tightened Lawson's face. "Dammit, why not?"

Wager smiled at him sympathetically. "It's better like this," he said. "You probably would have missed anyway. Less chance to embarrass yourself now."

Lawson snapped his gun back up. "You bastard, to hell with them. You're dead."

Then Lawson froze at the sound of a gun hammer being drawn. Behind him. John Nevers spoke gently and distinctly. "Mr. Skelly told you to put that gun down. I think you ought to do like he says."

Frustration and anger dueled for control of Lawson's face. The gun in his hand trembled dangerously. He glared at Wager down the barrel, then yanked the gun down to his side. "Soon, Wager," he hissed. "Don't you forget. Soon."

Lawson spun away, directing his rage at Skelly. "You better have a damned good reason for this."

"Go get Wager's horse," Skelly said. "He'll be riding along with us."

Nevers said, "I hope you don't mind my asking, but I don't

see the point of that either. Seems a whole lot simpler just to kill him now."

"Neither of you have seen this boat before," Skelly explained to his two gunmen. "It's like a fort. They could hole up in there and cause us a lot of grief trying to shoot our way in. Now, doesn't it sound a lot more pleasant if there's some way we can get them to come out and greet us? Like if they saw a friendly familiar face."

"Bait a trap for them, huh? Yeah, it makes sense."

"Sure, Johnson is an old trapper. He should appreciate the irony of it." Skelly turned to Wager. "I do hope you won't be a troublesome companion during the next few days. I would suggest you sit back and enjoy the trip."

"Right," Wager said sourly. "Like it's the last one I'll ever take."

"Good. I see we understand each other."

Wager had spent the majority of his life on hard-backed chairs, not in a saddle. The natural soreness he felt after two days on horseback was aggravated by the way they had him trussed up, with his hands tied to the pommel and his feet strapped to the cinch across the horse's belly. He was not able to use his leg muscles effectively to counter the shock of the horse's steps, so the result was a continual pounding to some of the most tender parts of his anatomy. Skelly's suggestion that he sit back and enjoy the trip stuck in his mind and soured.

It didn't help any that most of the journey was over some of the most rugged land in the whole Montana Territory. Wager could appreciate why the old man had chosen his sanctuary in such a place. There couldn't be many idle travelers willing to dare such landscape. On a few of the high mountain ledges and ridge-tops, Wager was almost glad for the added security of the ropes binding him. If he slid from the saddle he would find the drop a long, long one. Of course the other possibility, that of his horse stumbling and taking him along for the ride, did little to make the time pass swiftly.

He supposed he should be glad for that, since he might not have all that much time left. But it was difficult to see it quite that way.

On the easier stretches where they could ride alongside each other Skelly chattered at Wager continually, telling him one story after another. He seemed to appreciate having someone new for an audience, or maybe just the excuse for the telling of them, for he seemed to enjoy his own reminiscing more than any of them. Wager didn't mind listening; it helped to distract him from thoughts of what lay ahead, plus he was finally learning a few things about what the whole mess was about.

Skelly told him candidly about killing the Cornish family and how taking over their cattle empire had launched him into a career of wealth and influence. He showed no remorse at all about the past act of murder. To the contrary, he seemed quite pleased with himself, as if the killing had been an act of extraordinary resourcefulness. He said he had never known that Johnson had witnessed the family's murder. For twenty-some years Johnson had kept the secret to himself. Then one day, Skelly said, this young whippersnapper newspaperman showed up at his door claiming to be Ethan Johnson's son and presenting him with the whole story in print. Skelly told proudly of how he then set out again to eliminate an entire family, anyone, young or old, who might have heard the dark tale of his past.

"You see," Skelly said, "I am not like other men. They all look back on the past with regret, wishing that they had done something differently. But I create my past to suit my purposes. My life has proceeded exactly as I wish. I am probably the only man you will ever meet who has no regrets."

"Sure, you killed off everyone who remembers anything differently than you want it remembered."

"Exactly," Skelly said, as if Wager had given him a compliment. "But my life is much more than the past; it is truly just beginning. I have worked my way to the point where I can finally begin to reap the rich rewards I am due. The cattlemen's association are going to vote me in as their next president, Wager. And from that office it will be only a short step to the governorship. And from there . . . the sky is the limit. I am going to be a very big, big man. Do you know why?"

"Because you like to eat so much."

Skelly didn't laugh at that. "No, it's simply because I am not afraid. I want big things, and to get them I am willing to take big risks. I know the secret of success isn't talent, or skill, or even hard work. It's just daring, having the courage to do what has to be done. The big gamble. Hell, you should know that, Wager. What is it about you that makes you a good sharper? It's not flashy card tricks—lots of people can do card tricks, some of them better than any sharper—but a real gambler's got something extra: nerve. The nerve to use those card tricks without batting an eye, even though men are watching him close and there's big money on the table. That's what you got, Wager. And that's what I got, too. Maybe that's why I like you. We aren't so different, you and me."

"I don't gamble anymore," Wager said.

Skelly looked at him and cocked an eyebrow. "That's right. You lost your nerve, didn't you? Maybe that's why you're where you are now, and why I'm here."

Which was a thought, but not one Wager cared to dwell on.

They came to the river then. Skelly looked around and briefly consulted the crude maps in Johnson's diary. "Yes, this is it, all right," he said. "It hasn't changed a bit. All still exactly as I remember it." He gave Wager a broad smile. "It won't be long now."

"Swell," Wager said.


They came to a wide bend in the river and pulled up abruptly. Skelly motioned them back into the cover of the trees. "There it is, gentlemen."

The steamboat was faintly visible ahead, a splash of gray among the trees. The twin stacks rose starkly in the air. The stream of water that appeared under the pointed bow was about two yards narrower than the boat's hull. The sides were almost totally hidden by brushy undergrowth.

"What a dumb place for a boat," Lawson muttered. It was not a comment that deserved a reply, so no one said anything until Skelly climbed down from his horse, peered up the river for a minute, and finally nodded to himself as if coming to some decision. "Well, I can't see any reason why we shouldn't go ahead and get it over with." He smiled up at his prisoner. "Can you, Wager?"

"Only a few thousand."

# CHAPTER 28

THERE was nothing very involved about Skelly's plan. It was just simple enough to probably work, Wager thought grudgingly. Skelly sent Lawson and Nevers up ahead on foot, one on each side of the river. Then he stuck a gag in Wager's mouth.

"Resign yourself," Skelly said. "They're both going to die sooner or later. There's nothing you can do. If you try to run or do anything to warn them, John and Lawson will cut you down before you can take two steps. The longer you cooperate, the longer you all live." Then he slapped Wager's horse on the flank, sending him along the river. "Been nice knowing you, Wager."

Wager mumbled a scathing but totally unintelligible reply around his gag. It didn't seem to bother Skelly much.

The horse plodded slowly upstream, splashing through the shallows. With each step the steamboat loomed larger in his vision. He knew he was in plain sight now, if they were watching. He prayed they weren't. His only real hope was that maybe they wouldn't recognize him, or that they would smell the trap and stay in hiding, letting him ride right up to the boat. Once close enough to the boat, he could try to run for it. The boat would provide cover from Lawson's gun on the far side of the creek. He would just have to take his chances that Nevers would miss. As a plan, it had its drawbacks—mainly that it left him about as much chance of surviving as a snowball in hell.

Wager was about thirty yards from the boat when he saw a flash of motion on the deck. He knew then all bets were off. Sarah appeared at the rail, waving her arm wildly. "Sam! Sam, you found us," she cried, and the pleasure in her voice broke his heart wide open.

He shook his head savagely from side to side. But she wasn't watching. Sarah pounded down the gangplank and came running, splashing through the water with abandon, running to him as if nothing in the world could stop her. The glow in her eyes was something worth dying for.

In that instant Wager knew that was exactly what he had to do. Bound hand and foot, with his voice stilled, he had but one option. He took it without hesitation.

As Sarah grew nearer, he suddenly dug his knees viciously into the horse's sides, urging it into a run. The horse bolted forward.

Two shots boomed.

The world tilted crazily as Wager's horse screamed and tumbled in its tracks, dragging him down with it. He tugged helplessly at his bonds as the animal rolled onto its side in a river of blood. Wager had but a split second to draw in a breath, then the dark water closed over his head.

Panic seized him, and he struggled frantically to lift his head. The surface of the water was only inches away, but the binding held him short. Already the air was bubbling through his lips, a tight hunger growing in his chest.

He could see the sunlight shimmering on the water's surface so clearly, so near. The bubbles of his passing life rising to burst there, to vanish before his eyes.

Then the water shuddered and a shadowy shape blotted the sun.

And Sarah was there. She pulled out the gag and her arms closed around him, lifting his head a critical few inches.

Wager tasted the air's dryness, gasping with a sound as sharp as an infant's first cry. He drew in life hungrily, swelling his chest with its dizzy sweetness.

Sarah braced a knee below his back while her hands groped, exploring. She found the rope at his wrists, legs. The familiar skinning knife appeared in her hand. "I'll have to drop you back under," she said.

Wager shook his head. "No, go on, Sarah. It's a trap. Run."

She said nothing, just yanked her hand away, and suddenly Wager plunged back into the water. He felt the panic twist at his gut, but it was only a second before his hands pulled free and he rose sputtering to the air again. A moment later Sarah reappeared from below. She wrapped her arms around him, and together they strained and pulled until his leg tugged free from below the horse's weight. They crawled to the bank and collapsed in each other's arms.

"Dammit, why didn't you run?" Wager gasped.

"You won't get rid of me that easy, Sam Wager," she said, and wrapped her arms even tighter. Wager did likewise, and for a moment they pressed against each other as if trying to join in one skin.

"Now, ain't that a touching sight. You two know each other?"

With a soft groan, Wager rolled from Sarah and glared up at the man standing over them. "Damn you, Nevers."

"Real snappy, Wager."

Sarah sat up beside him, still hugging him close. They both took in the sight of Lawson directly across the river, Skelly on horseback just a short way downstream. The big man smiled once down at them, then stood up in the stirrups and cupped his hands to his mouth. "Give it up, Johnson," he yelled. "Throw your guns out and show yourself. Surrender now or watch the girl die."

The old man appeared from behind a crate on the boat deck. Slowly, he walked to the bow. He shook his gray head, then tossed his rifle into the river. "I should have killed you a long time ago. Skelly," he said. "A whole long time ago."

And just like that, it was over.

# CHAPTER 29

SKELLY rode up slowly until he could grin down at Wager. "You tried, at least, didn't you?"

"Yeah."

"Well, that's something."

Wager was still sitting in the mud with his arms around Sarah. He leaned back and looked up at the fat man. "Kill me now if you're going to, Skelly. Just don't make me listen to any more of your garbage."

Skelly studied him a moment, then flicked the reins and rode on past. "Bring them up to the boat," he said to Nevers.

The gunman nudged Wager in the small of his back with the rifle. "You heard him. Get moving."

Wager climbed up on one knee, reached out to help Sarah stand. As his hand went to her waist, he felt a small lump in her coat pocket. It reminded him of something, and as he pulled her to her feet, he gently reached into the pocket and grabbed a handful of the crystals.

"Sam?" Sarah said, flinching. A look from him stilled further protests.

Nevers was standing a few feet behind them, the rifle held casually in one hand. He clucked his tongue at Wager in a sorrowful noise. "That woman of yours seems a bit ticklish. Appears you ain't done much to break her in right."

"You're right, Nevers. Who needs her." With that, Wager roughly pushed Sarah to one side. As the gunman's eyes narrowed in surprise, Wager kicked him hard in the shin. Nevers's mouth opened in a sharp gasp of pain. In that moment, Wager tossed the crystals full in his face, then made a grab for the rifle.

184

The muddy riverbank was a poor place to try it. Wager's foot slipped as he launched himself, and his reach fell inches short. Nevers yanked the gun clear easily, then swung it around and cracked the barrel across Wager's shoulders. Wager dropped to his hands and knees, stunned.

"You son of a bitch!" Nevers sputtered, backing up a step and spitting angrily. The white powder covered his face like a dusting of sugar, and he grimaced as he wiped a hand across his chin. "You're gonna be real sorry you tried that," he said. "By the time I'm through with you, you'll be begging to die."

Sarah dropped beside Wager and helped him up again. He held her close. "I'm sorry, Sarah. I didn't mean it."

"I know," she said quietly.

They held each other as Nevers marched them up to the boat. Skelly stood at the top of the gangplank with Johnson by his side. Lawson hung just behind the old man. He had his gun in hand, but wasn't bothering to point it anywhere. Johnson didn't look to be giving them any trouble. His shoulders sagged, his head hung low, and he seemed to have shrunk, collapsed in on himself. His eyes peered from sunken sockets, dull, without light.

Nevers prodded Sarah and Wager up the plank. They silently took their place beside the old man. Sarah looked concernedly up at Johnson, but he kept staring at nothing, or at something none of the others could see.

Skelly stared at Nevers's face a moment. "Wager give you some trouble?"

Nevers spat on the deck. "No, no trouble at all."

The fat man shrugged and turned to Sarah. "I wish I could say the same for you, girl. You've been nothing but trouble for a long time now. You made a good run of it, but the end was inevitable. You could have done us all a big favor by giving up back when it all started."

Wager said, "You could do us a favor by saving all the chatter."

"Bitter, Wager?" Skelly said, smiling. "I thought you were a bigger man than that."

"You haven't been right about anything yet."

"This is my moment of triumph. You must permit me to enjoy it in my own way." Skelly turned to Johnson. "And I must congratulate you, old man, for choosing this place for our final meeting. Yes, a most fitting place." He motioned toward the wheelhouse high above them. "You and the captain's woman, together in death. You can lie with her forever, as you always wanted."

"Leave him alone," Sarah cried. "Haven't you hurt him enough?"

Skelly ignored her, his eyes locked on the cowering old trapper. "You crazy old fool. You know, there was a time when I almost admired you. But it all ended here, didn't it? Now everything ends here."

Johnson didn't react. He seemed not even to hear, as if he were beyond hearing anything, or caring.

Skelly looked around at them all and frowned, as if disappointed. He made a short gesture at Nevers. "All right. Finish it."

"Just a minute," Lawson broke in. He pushed forward, his eyes flashing in a leering smile. "The girl's mine, remember. I been chasing her the better part of a year, and now I want what's coming for all that bother. And she's gonna make it all up to me."

Skelly's lip curled. "Lawson, you truly are disgusting."

"What's that, fat man?"

The two men glared at each other for a moment; then Skelly turned away and made a brief dismissive motion. "Oh, very well. Take her."

"No," a low voice said firmly.

They all turned in wonder toward the old man. Johnson's head was up; his dull, lifeless eyes stared right at Lawson. "No," he said softly. "I won't let that happen."

The gunman tipped back his head and laughed. "How you

plan to stop me?" His hand arched up and a shot drove Johnson reeling backwards.

"No!" Sarah screamed. She broke free from Wager and ran the few steps to grab at Johnson as he fell. She locked her arms around him and tried to hold him up, but his weight bore them both to the deck. Slowly, she pulled her hand back and stared at the blood dripping from her fingers.

Wager tensed, but before he could move, a gun jabbed him in the spine. "Stay out of it," Nevers said. "You just watch."

Sarah moved faster than any of them could follow. With a wild cry of agony, she pulled her knife and launched herself at the gloating gunman. Lawson barely managed to swing his arm up, deflecting the lunging blade. A thin red line streaked his open palm. He hissed in pain and snapped his hand up, striking Sarah across the face before she could draw back for another lunge. The blow jerked her head back, dazing her. Lawson twisted the knife free and caught her by the wrist. He gave a vicious yank, nearly pulling her off her feet. "You're gonna be real sorry you did that, girl," he growled. "You're gonna pay for that in ways you can't even . . ." His voice died abruptly as his eyes focused on something past her, something they didn't believe.

Lawson shoved her aside and shrank back against the wall as Johnson came at him.

All the witnesses drew back in a kind of horror at the sight of the old man. His shirt was red with blood, and he moved with a lurching shuffle, as if dragging himself on by sheer force of will.

Lawson's gun spat fire twice more. Johnson's body bucked, temporarily halted by the bullets slamming him back. But he kept his feet. Relentlessly, he stumbled forward, closing on the gunman as if nothing in the world could stop him.

Lawson's gun clicked on dry chambers. As the huge, powerful hands closed on his throat, he screamed.

"Get away from me! Let go, you crazy bastard, dammit . . . you're dead!"

Johnson's voice was like a dry wind moaning through a cold, lonely canyon. "I know," he said. And he was smiling.

Lawson clawed frantically at the hands locked around his neck. His eyes bulged and his mouth opened in a scream, but nothing sounded. Johnson's fingers buried themselves in his neck, pushing him against the wall, lifting him clear off his feet. A shudder passed through the old man, and for a second he seemed to falter. Then he collected himself and pressed harder, raising Lawson to full arm's length, so that the gunman was supported in the air by nothing but that terrible, unrelenting grip. There was a snap like the splitting of a dry tree in a gusting wind, and Lawson's head swung to one side, the eyes open and empty.

Johnson sighed softly. The shuddering rippled through him again, and he slowly settled to the floor, pulling Lawson with him, refusing to let go, his grip as strong as death itself. Peacefully, he closed his eyes.

In the silence that followed, Wager slowly walked over and took Sarah's hand. There were tears on her face, but her expression was one of pride.

Skelly shook himself as if out of a trance. "Damn," he muttered. "Who would have believed the old fool had it in him. Damn."

Wager said softly, "Makes you wonder, doesn't it? Big man."

Skelly pursed his lips and nodded in a grudging fashion. "He died well, Wager. Maybe better than he lived. Now, how about you, how well can you die? You ready to learn?"

"I'm not all that curious."

"Too bad."

# CHAPTER 30

NEVERS had a very sour look on his face. "Let's stop talking and get it done," he said.

Skelly seemed amused. "What's the matter, John? Does all this killing leave a bad taste in your mouth?"

"Ain't that. I'm just tired."

Skelly turned to his two prisoners. "He does have a point, I'm afraid. There is really no reason to postpone this any longer."

Wager and Sarah stood with their arms around each other. "At least we'll be together, Sam," she whispered. "I believe that."

Skelly laughed. "Sure you will. Just like Johnson and the captain's woman."

Sarah scowled. "What do you mean?"

"Didn't the old fool tell you that story about the woman he met here?"

"Sure," Sarah said. "She died out there on the river. Wolves got her."

"He told you that?"

"Of course. That's what happened."

A gleam of amusement sparkled in Skelly's eyes. "Come with me, girl. There's something I want you to see." He grabbed Sarah's arm and pulled her along.

"Where are you taking her?" Wager demanded.

"Not far," Skelly said. He glanced back at Nevers. The gunman's eyes were distant, lethargic. "What's the matter with you?"

"Nothing," Nevers grumbled. "Just hurry it up."

"You keep an eye on Wager. This won't take long."

Skelly dragged Sarah across the foredeck and crossed over to the port side. They came to the ladder leading up to the upper deck and the wheelhouse. "Climb it," Skelly ordered.

Sarah glanced up fearfully. "I don't want to go up there."

Skelly jabbed the gun roughly into her back. "Nobody asked what you wanted. Climb."

Wager was watching Nevers closely. The gunman's eyes were fluttering, and he was breathing in rapid gasps. "You sure you're all right?" Wager asked.

Nevers waved his gun about. "Mind your own business."

"You sure don't look all right."

Nevers glared at Wager and raised his gun. "The hell with Skelly. I'm going to finish you now."

Wager tensed his muscles, preparing to dive at the gunman. It would be a hopeless move, but he sure wasn't going to just stand there and take it.

But at that moment the first spasm hit Nevers. His hand went to his throat, and his mouth emitted a low gurgling noise. His eyes grew wide with panic, but his pupils were moving from side to side uncontrollably. He bent over, gasping for breath, but then his entire body sprang out straight like a bow as the arrow is released. He tipped over backwards and crashed to the deck, his spine arching and straightening in rapid seizures.

Wager bolted over and tried to pull away the gun. It was like trying to pull it from the jaws of a grizzly. Nevers's whole body kept hopping away from him, thrashing about in one violent spasm after another. As Wager fought to break the grip of those convulsed fingers, the gun went off, the bullet burying itself in the deck.

"Hey, what's going on down there!"

Wager glanced hurriedly over his shoulder, saw Skelly leaning out from the roof overhead. The big man hurriedly snapped off a shot, the bullet whistling past Wager, just wide. Just wide enough so that it struck Nevers in the chest. Blood spurted, and the gunman's body jerked again, pulling the gun from Wager's hand.

Another shot from overhead spit up chips of wood from the deck, inches from Wager's head. Nevers's body kept flopping about the deck like a landed fish, and Wager knew he could never pull that gun free in time. Then his eyes fell on his own gun, still stuck in Nevers's waistband, where it had been ever since Nevers had taken it from Wager. Damning himself for a fool, Wager dove out and yanked the gun free.

Skelly fired again, but Wager didn't see where the shot went. Rolling quickly on his back, he fired two hurried shots that probably were nowhere close. But they did the trick, making Skelly back away and out of sight.

Without hesitation, Wager ran to the opposite side, leaped up, and grabbed the railing of the middle deck. Even when he was a boy and in full practice from shinnying trees, he could not have climbed any faster. He threw himself over the railing and crouched in the shadows, listening with every fiber of his being for a sound from above.

Nothing. The silence seemed to drag out forever. All he could hear was the pounding of his own heart.

Wager realized the deck he stood on was only seven or eight feet below the level of the wheelhouse. He knew there was a protective footrail around the top deck. It would make a convenient handhold. Gauging these distances, he knew what he had to do.

Carefully so as to make no noise of his own, he stepped up onto the railing. He balanced himself on the wooden beam by crouching and bracing one hand and the top of his head against the overhead. The railing brought him up another three feet so that if he straightened to his full height, he could rear up head and shoulders above the edge of the top deck.

High enough to get off a shot. Or to be a good target.

It was a matter of picking the right place to poke up his head. Slowly, he shuffled along the rail until he was well down the starboard side, directly opposite the ladder that led to the top deck. The ladder would have to be the place Skelly watched closest. But still Wager had no clue as to where the big man might be waiting. He could easily pop his head up and find himself at Skelly's feet.

But there was nothing else to try. Muttering a silent oath, he grabbed quickly for the footrail and slung himself out and up.

He saw Skelly at once. The big man was at the stern end of the upper deck, where he could scan its entire length and breadth. He held Sarah in front of him like a shield.

Skelly saw him and cried out in surprise. He snapped off a shot that pinged off the footrail, making it vibrate in Wager's hand. He had no shot, not with Sarah so close. He swung himself back and dropped to the middle deck.

Wager was running even as he touched the floor. He knew now there was only one way to the top, one place where he might climb up protected, and he had to get there before Skelly had the same thought.

His boots pounded as he ran back around to the center of the deck. There was just a chance that he could climb up, keeping the wheelhouse between him and Skelly. But if Skelly thought to move to one side, it would be like plunking ducks as they bob to the surface of a lake.

Wager didn't give himself time to think about it. He reached the point he figured was center, and he jumped up on the railing again, grabbed the rail, and slung himself up and over.

He rolled onto the top deck with his heart in his throat. But no shots sounded. He raced the two steps and flung himself down against the wall of the wheelhouse, wondering which side Skelly would appear on.

But no figure jumped into view. After a moment, Wager cautiously peered around the corner of the small structure.

Skelly had not moved. He still stood dead-center at the stern railing. Only his gun had changed position. He had it pointed straight at Sarah's head.

"Give it up, Wager," Skelly called. "I know you're there. Give it up and throw your gun out. Or the next shot blows the girl away."

Wager ducked back out of sight. There was still no shot;

Skelly held Sarah too close. He couldn't risk it, not from the full length of the boat.

"We're waiting, Wager. Throw it out now or I shoot her."

"You kill her, you've got no more protection," Wager called. "Let her go and we'll go at it, man to man, just you and me."

Skelly's laugh boomed. "No, I like the odds better the way they are."

"It's a standoff. Let her go."

"No draws," Skelly yelled. "In this game there's gotta be a winner."

"You can't kill her, Skelly. If you do, nothing in the world will stop me from getting you."

Skelly laughed harshly. "That's just noise. Come out now, Wager. A dead body is still shield enough."

Wager blinked. Something in the back of his mind made a connection. Then he remembered. With sudden conviction, he broken open the revolver. There were four live shells left. He removed the two spent shells, hesitated, then took out two of the live ones. Carefully, he closed the gun and spun the cylinder to the first of the empty chambers.

Okay, Skelly, he thought, let's see who's still got some nerve.

Then he stood up and walked around the wheelhouse.

# CHAPTER 31

AT the sight of Wager, Sarah struggled to break free of Skelly's hold. He dropped his hand from her mouth to get a better grip around her.

"Sam, no!" Sarah cried.

Wager walked slowly forward, the gun held straight out before him. Skelly laughed derisively. "You won't take the shot. You can't risk it. You won't chance hitting the girl."

"Do it, Sam. Try it," Sarah said. "You've got to; he'll kill me anyway."

Wager said nothing, kept walking.

"That's far enough," Skelly warned. His thumb drew back the gun's hammer. "One more step and the girl dies."

Wager stopped. He held the gun out, but made no apparent effort at aiming. "You're right," he said. "This is close enough."

Skelly growled, "All right. Now drop the gun."

"No," Sarah screamed. "Do it. Take the shot!"

Wager nodded. And pulled the trigger.

The gun clicked dry on the empty chamber.

"Bang," Wager said. The gun clicked three more times, hollowly.

There was nothing else in the world for him but Sarah's eyes. The look in them was almost too much to bear. "My God, no," she said. "Not again. Not another empty gun."

Wager shrugged. "You remember how I hate loud noises."

Skelly shook his head. "Damn, you tried to play a bluff. Damned bluff."

"What the hell," Wager sighed.

Sarah's voice was pure venom. "You fool, you've killed us both."

If there was any doubt in Skelly's mind, Sarah's sudden anger convinced him. He looked at Wager and laughed. "She's sure right about you. You dumb bastard, don't you know you can't bluff in a gunfight? You sure learn your lessons the hard way, don't you? Well, this lesson's your last."

With a gloating smile, Skelly pushed Sarah to one side and brought his gun to bear on Wager. "That was the dumbest bet you ever made."

Wager fired. One bullet took Skelly in the chest, the second right in his open mouth. The force of the blows drove him straight off the deck. His body dropped onto one of the paddle-wheel spokes, perched there a second, then slid slowly down to the water. A stream of red bubbled and quickly disappeared under the stern.

Wager turned away. He had seen all he needed to see. Sarah came into his arms. They kissed, and it was everything else that he needed.

After a long moment, he gently pushed her away. "We've got some graves to dig," he said.

Sarah shook her head. "Just one. For Ethan." She looked off down the river and quietly added, "Leave the others out. For the wolves to find."

Wager frowned. "I still don't know what you got against wolves."


They buried Johnson on a high glade a little way from the river, facing east so, as Sarah said, he could watch the sun rise over his beloved mountains. Wager fashioned a crude cross from planks taken from the boat. On it he scratched a simple epitaph:

ETHAN JOHNSON
HE LIVED PROUD, AND DIED WITH NO REGRETS


Sarah told him it was perfect. She placed a bouquet of

wildflowers at the base of the cross; then they linked arms and walked away, without another word.

Just before they left, Wager climbed to the top deck once more. He went to the window of the wheelhouse and rubbed a hand at the grime and dust collected there until he had cleared a space to peer through. The two skeletons were sitting side by side with their arms around each other. The big one had a hole in the center of its skull. The small one had none.

Wager turned and climbed back down. Sarah never asked him what he saw, and he never offered to tell her.

# CHAPTER 32

THEY had one more burial to perform. They laid the boy to rest in the shade of the pines by Johnson's cabin. Then they rode together into Sheridan. Wager sensed one or two men looking at them with more than usual interest, but no one bothered them. Finally, they ran into Dr. Michael Court. "Come back to settle your bill, did you, Wager?" the man said with a smile.

"I owe you a lot more than I can repay."

Court brushed that off with a wave of his hand. "Money's always been good enough for me."

"How are things here, Doc?" Wager asked. "Am I riding back into more trouble?"

"Naw, nobody cares, nobody remembers. The new sheriff went through some of the paperwork and found that Price fellow you killed was wanted. His first official act as sheriff was to accept the bounty. He'll want to thank you, maybe buy you a drink and bore you to death with his jabber. But that's as bad as you can expect from him. Your friend Lon Do and I will vouch for you if anyone else tries to raise a stink. I don't think you need to worry."

"Thanks, Doc. You can't know how that makes me feel."

Court shook his head and smiled. "No, I don't imagine I can. Can I?"

When Wager awoke, Sarah was standing by the window. The morning sun glistened on her skin so that she almost seemed to glow. Her body was a statue of pastels, lines and shadows somehow softer than reality.

Her head was tilted to the light. Like a flower, he thought, like a wildflower seeking the sun.

He watched her, feeling a tug at his heart. He understood something all too well now. She was indeed a wild thing, as free and natural as the creatures in the wilderness she loved. A man could touch her, but she could not be held, not for long. If he tried to possess her, something inside her would perish.

She turned then and saw him watching her. She smiled and came back to the bed, climbed in beside him. "Sam?"

"I know," he said gently.

"Hold me once more before I go."

He agreed that was a fine idea.


Afterward, Wager went downstairs while she dressed and gathered her belongings. He drank the coffee Do brought him and fiddled with a deck of cards while he waited. One-handed poker. He dealt out five cards without looking at them.

Then she was there.

"I'm sorry, Sam," she said softly. "You know I don't belong here." She tossed her head back and bit her lip. "My place is out there, at the cabin, doing the work Ethan taught me."

"Carrying on."

"Yes."

"Well, four miles isn't all that far," he said. "I might enjoy a little ride now and then."

"Soon," she said.

"Often."

Wager flipped over the cards he had dealt himself. It was a full house. He frowned.

Sarah leaned over his shoulder and let out a small sigh. "Aces and eights. The dead man's hand?"

Wager picked up one of the eights and threw it off the table. Then, in a blur of motion, he cut one-handed and dealt off the top card. He slid the last ace in next to the others. "There, that's better."

Sarah shook her head. "How did you do that?"
Wager smiled. "Just lucky, I guess."

If you have enjoyed this book and would like to receive details of other Walker Western titles, please write to:

Western Editor
Walker and Company
720 Fifth Avenue
New York, NY 10019